Upgraded To Wifey Status:

Goo & Candy's Story

By: Twyla T. & Patrice Balark

Upgraded To Wifey Status: Goo & Candy's Story

MAILING LIST

ARE YOU ON THE LIST?

<u>CLICK HERE</u> To join Cole Hart Presents' mailing list and receive new book release alerts, exclusive giveaways, sneak peeks & more!

Receive instant new book release alerts by texting Cole Hart to 42828

BOOKS BY TWYLA T.

My Thug, My Savage, My Dope Boy

My Thug, My Savage, My Dope Boy 2

Thug Holiday

Thug Holiday 2

Thug Holiday 3

Pretty Lips That Thugs Love: An Urban Romance

Pretty Lips That Thugs Love 2: An Urban Romance

Pretty Lips That Thugs Love 3: An Urban Romance

Pretty Lips That Thugs Love 4: An Urban Romance

My Shawty: An Original Love Story

My Shawty 2: An Original Love Story

My Shawty 3: An Original Love Story

Queens of Urban Fiction

The Wife Of A Kingpin

The Wife Of A Kingpin 2: Malik & Micah's Story

The Wife Of A Kingpin 3: Malik & Micah's Story

We Both Can't Be Bae

We Both Can't Be Bae 2

We Both Can't Be Bae 3

I'll Never Love A Dope Boy Again: An Urban Fiction Romance

I'll Never Love A Dope Boy Again 2

BOOKS BY PATRICE BALARK

A Secret Hood Love

A Secret Hood Love Affair 2

Thug Holiday

Thug Holiday 2

Thug Holiday 3

Black Tonya: A Women's Fiction Novel

Black Tonya 2: An Urban Romance

Lovin' A Chi-Town Kingpin

Lovin' A Chi-Town Kingpin 2

The Wife Of A Kingpin

The Wife Of A Kingpin 2: Malik & Micah's Story

The Wife Of A Kingpin 3: Malik & Micah's Story

BOOKS BY COLE HART PRESENTS

ANNA BLACK

Sometimes I'm In My Feelings: An Urban Romance

Sometimes I'm In My Feelings 2: An Urban Romance

Queens of Urban Fiction

B. RICHEMOND

Hood Luv In Miami

CACHET

This Could Be Us But You Playin'

This Could Be Us But You Playin' 2

This Could Be Us But You Playin' 3

CHASE SIDORA AND SOL

Ace & Bleu: A Dope Boy Love Story

Ace & Bleu 2: A Dope Boy Love Story

COLE HART

I Need A Fiancée Like Beyonce

I Like My Women BBW

Rich Thugs

I'm Low Key Feeling You 2: The Finale

DANI LITTLEPAGE

Just Like The Rest of 'Em: A Dopeboy Love Story

Just Like The Rest of 'Em 2: A Dopeboy Love Story

My Other Baby Mama: A Dope Boy Saga

My Other Baby Mama 2: A Dope Boy Saga

Thug Holiday

Thug Holiday 2

Thug Holiday 3

DANIELLE MARCUS

Thug Kisses: An Urban Romance Story

Thug Kisses 2: An Urban Romance Story

J. DOMINIQUE

Red and Ricko: A Dope Boy Original: A Urban Fiction Romance

Red and Ricko 2

Red & Ricko 3: A Dope Boy Love Story

Thug Holiday

A Secret Hood Love Affair 2

Thug Holiday

Thug Holiday 2

Thug Holiday 3

Black Tonya: A Women's Fiction Novel

Black Tonya 2: An Urban Romance

Lovin' A Chi-Town Kingpin

Lovin' A Chi-Town Kingpin 2

The Wife Of A Kingpin

The Wife Of A Kingpin 2: Malik & Micah's Story

The Wife Of A Kingpin 3: Malik & Micah's Story

PRINCESS DIAMOND

Dream and Drake: A Cartel Love Story

Dream and Drake 2: A Cartel Love Story

Dream and Drake 3: A Cartel Love Story

Dream and Drake 4: A Cartel Love Story

Everybody Got A Secret: An Urban Romance

Everybody Got A Secret 2: An Urban Romance

Everybody Got A Secret 3: An Urban Romance

Everybody Got A Secret 4: An Urban Romance

A King Pin Stole My Heart: An Original Love Story

SANDRA NICOLE

Weekends Only

TASHA MACK

Angel & Dante: A Dopeboy Love Story

TWYLA T.

My Thug, My Savage, My Dope Boy

My Thug, My Savage, My Dope Boy 2

Thug Holiday

Thug Holiday 2

Thug Holiday 3

Pretty Lips That Thugs Love: An Urban Romance

Pretty Lips That Thugs Love 2: An Urban Romance

Pretty Lips That Thugs Love 3: An Urban Romance

Pretty Lips That Thugs Love 4: An Urban Romance

My Shawty: An Original Love Story

My Shawty 2: An Original Love Story

My Shawty 3: An Original Love Story

Queens of Urban Fiction

The Wife Of A Kingpin

The Wife Of A Kingpin 2: Malik & Micah's Story

The Wife Of A Kingpin 3: Malik & Micah's Story

__Text__ TwylaT __to__ 21000 __to stay up to date on new releases, plus get information on contests, sneak peeks, and more!!!!__

Dedication

This series is dedicated to Cardi B. If you work hard for what you want, nothing or no one can stop you! The come up is real!! Thanks for the inspiration, Belcalis Almanzar!!

Acknowledgements

God!!

Other Great Reads By Twyla T.

We Both Can't Be Bae 1-3

I'll Never Love A Dope Boy Again 1 & 2

My Shawty 1-3 (An Original Love Story)

Pretty Lips That Thugs Love 1-4

The Wife Of A Kingpin 1-3 (Collab with Patrice Balark)

Thug Holiday 1-3 (Collaboration)

My Thug, My Savage, My Dope Boy 1-2

Facebook, Instagram, and Twitter handles are all @authortwylat

You may also email me at authortwylat@gmail.com and check out my website authortwylat.com

Search Loyal T's Clique on Facebook if you love my work and become a

supporter! We love to kick back and have fun in there, and there also random giveaways!

Other Great Reads By Patrice Balark

Lovin' A Chi-Town Kingpin 1-2

Black Tonya 1-2

The Wife of a Kingpin 1-3 (Collab with Twyla T.)

Thug Holiday 1-3 (Collaboration)

Chapter 1

Goo sat in the back of *Structure's* in a VIP section he reserved just for him and his team and scoped out the place. It was a Saturday night, so you know it was lit. There were bottles flowing, weed smoke polluting the air while bad bitches scattered around like roaches did in the projects when you cut the lights on. The vibe was decent, and the DJ kept the latest hits spinning while the niggaz in there did all they could do to catch the attention of the ladies who was looking for a quick come up. Usually, the strip club was one of Goo's *"things"* but lately, his mind was on getting money, nothing more and nothing less. Truth be told, he was only there that night because his homie Malik was back in the city from his honeymoon in Paris. It had been two weeks since he had seen his right-hand man, and they had some catching up to do.

"Fuck you sitting here looking lost for?"

Goo looked up and laughed at Malik who had finally arrived.

"My nigga, I ain't think you was coming," he said, standing to his feet and greeting him with a handshake that turned into a manly hug.

"I told yo ass I would be here," Malik replied, looking around the crowded club.

"Nah, I'm just saying... I thought maybe Micah made you stay home," Goo stated.

"Yo ass sound crazy. I'm a grown ass man, Micah knows that," Malik bragged.

"Yeah, yeah, yeah... I bet yo ass got a curfew or better yet, she gave you a beeper didn't she? Did yo ass like Gina did Martin the day they came back from their honeymoon," Goo laughed.

"Yo ass stay with the jokes. I give you about three months and Candy gon' have yo ass on curfew too," Malik joined in on the laughter.

The duo shared a few more jokes before sitting down on the plush gray couches. After about fifteen minutes, their section was filled with members of their crew. Although smoking in that establishment wasn't allowed, Goo flamed up a blunt anyway, clearly not giving a fuck about the possible repercussions.

I been movin' calm, don't start no trouble with me
Tryna keep it peaceful is a struggle for me
Don't pull up at 6 AM to cuddle with me
You know how I like it when you lovin' on me
I don't wanna die for them to miss me
Yes I see the things that they wishin' on me
Hope I got some brothers that outlive me
They gon' tell the story, shit was different with me

Drake's latest single, *Gods Plan,* blasted through the speakers, causing everyone to go crazy. Goo, never been a fan of Drake's music, slightly bobbed his head up and down, rapping along in his mind. He couldn't front, the song was catchy as fuck, but he was more into rappers like Jeezy, who rapped about trap shit, actual shit he could relate to. It had been a minute since him and his guys kicked it. The past year, they had gone through so much shit. Beefing with niggaz they didn't even know they *had* beef with. Sending a few niggaz to the grave and dealing with rats that were in their own circle. They didn't have time to chill because niggaz would take advantage as soon as they were caught lacking.

As soon as the song ended, Goo felt his phone vibrate in his pocket. He reached inside his Balmain jeans and retrieved the iPhone 7. There were a few missed calls and a couple of unread text messages. He glanced at the call log, not seeing a call of importance, he then went to his text messages. There was two that stood out to him: one from Candy and another one from this chick named Nicki.

Candy: I love you be safe.

Nicki: I need some dick... make your way.

Goo replied to Candy's message, leaving Nicki's on read. Although the drama had died down, he wasn't really focusing on bitches right now. As a matter of fact, they had seemed to be the root of his problems. Goo married who he *thought* was the love of his life at a young age. Mona had the looks, the hustler's mentality, and most importantly, she kept her mouth closed. She knew all about the life Goo led. He showered her with everything a girl could want and in return, she held him down, or so he thought. Turned out, Mona was tired of Goo's infidelity, and she stepped out on him. It wasn't the cheating that bothered Goo, it was the person she cheated with. Not only did Mona get involved with Bear, one of Goo's enemies, she got pregnant by him and tried to pin the baby on Goo. Once the smoke cleared and everything was uncovered, the both of them, Bear and Mona, ended up together, living happily ever after from their graves. During the time Goo was married to Mona, he was involved with many chicks, but he *only* considered one very special, and that was Candy. Candy was different than the fake bougie hood bitches he was used to. As a matter of fact, Candy was an attorney and a good girl. When Goo got into a jam, due to being set up by Mona, Candy came through and handled shit, ultimately winning him over for good; that and the fact she gave him his first born.

"You gon' look at yo phone all night or you gon' let me show you a good time?"

Goo looked up and stared at a tall, chocolate beautiful woman, wearing nothing but a bra, some cut up shorts, and licked his lips. There were plenty of bitches in the club, but her unique beauty made her stand out like a sore thumb.

"I would shorty, but I'm chilling right now," he finally answered.

"Oh ok," she pouted, poking out her bottom lip before turning and walking away.

It wasn't until then that Goo got a glimpse of that ass and instantly regretted his decision.

"Aye!" he said, reaching out to her, grabbing her arm, and pulling her back.

The beautiful woman turned around wearing a smile that could light up a room.

"I thought you'll change your mind, follow me," she ordered, leading Goo out of the VIP section through the maroon curtains that led to the back rooms.

Once in the back, they entered the third room on the right. Behind the door was an orange couch, a small stage, and the lighting was extremely dim. The shit that went down in these rooms was endless, and with Candy in the back of his head, he knew that he was about to do something that would have him apologizing later.

"Aye shorty, I ain't even get yo name," Goo said, flopping down on the couch while the young lady walked over to the pole that was in the middle of the stage.

"Ohhh my name? That's not gon' matter because you're not going to remember it," she said in a flirty tone.

"How the fuck you gon' tell me what Ima remember?" he asked as she twirled around on the pole.

"Because... dead niggaz have bad memories," she blurted out, pulling a .22 out of her shorts and pointing it at Goo.

Goo looked at her and laughed. Not the least bit worried or concerned.

"Who sent yo dumb ass off?" he inquired.

"Nigga, I'm asking the questions," she yelled, walking closer to him with the gun still aimed in his direction.

"First of all, you need to lower your voice and then lower your gun," he stated.

"And if I don't?" she asked, letting out a cocky chuckle before one bullet went into the back of her head, causing her lifeless body to hit the ground.

"Then that's gon' happen," Goo stood up and said, stepped over her body, and walked to the door where Malik stood.

"What you doing here?" Goo asked.

"Nigga, apparently saving yo life," Malik shot back.

"Nigga, I was good," Goo lied.

"Let you tell it, now let's get the fuck outta here," Malik said, turning around to leave out.

"But how did you know about shorty?" Goo questioned.

"She been scoping us out since we got here....."

"I knew that,." Goo cut him off.

"Nigga, you ain't know shit," Malik laughed.

The two of them left from the back but not before Malik whispered something to the bouncer, who shook his head in agreeance. The both of them knew it was time to go before something else went down, but before that thought could leave their minds, gun shots rang out from the front of the club. Both Goo and Malik ran over to where their crew was and returned the gun fire until they were the only ones shooting. Apparently, whoever sent the stripper bitch noticed Goo and Malik leaving out. They knew that their messenger had failed, so they decided to take matters in their own hands and start a shootout. Just when Goo thought shit was dying down for him and his team, here they were, back into the street shit. I guess the saying is true, *there's only two ways out, either jail or the grave.*

Chapter 2

After Candy packed RJ's bag, she brushed her hair up into a high ponytail and admired herself in the full-length mirror. Her snapback had been real, and she was grateful. Candy had packed on a good forty pounds while pregnant, but it fell off with the quickness along. Goo had often teased her and said *he missed her big ass breasts*, but she shrugged his comments off.

"Ma... ma," RJ called out, and it made Candy's heart melt as she turned around and smiled at him.

"Hey mama's baby... here I come."

His birthday was quickly approaching, and Candy had already started planning his party. She hurriedly finished up and picked him up, along with his bag, her phone, keys, and headed out of the door after putting on both of their coats. It was cold as fuck, but there wasn't any snow on the ground mid-January, which the people of Chicago were thankful for. Goo was out with Malik, and she was headed to meet up with her girl Micah. Malik had taken her on a two-week long honeymoon, and Candy had been missing her boo. She cruised the streets and was thankful that the traffic was light. Twenty minutes later, she pulled up at the home of the Jeffersons.

Candy sent Micah a text to let her know that she was outside before she gathered RJ up and got out. As soon as she made it to the door, it swung open.

"Heeyyy!" her and Micah squealed at each other in unison.

"Give me my baby... he's getting *sooo* big," Micah took RJ from her.

"He greedy like his damn daddy," Candy laughed as she followed Micah to the living room and sat down on the chaise.

"So what I been missing in the city?" Micah asked.

"Girl, nothing. Please believe me, I would have traded places with you in a heartbeat," Candy rolled her eyes.

"Well... it's time for you and Goo to make it official, so I can keep RJ while y'all honeymoon."

"Whatever... I love Goo, but that nigga *ain't* ready for marriage. Mona's ass did a number on him," Candy replied as she thought back to Goo's ex who was now dead. She had caused so much shit before she died that it did a number on Goo.

Candy thought back to how she had fallen in love with Goo before she even knew he was married. Their relationship was complicated, and she even broke up with his ass while she was pregnant, but Goo wouldn't go away easily. His ex-wife, Mona, had set him up and had him locked up, but thankfully Candy, along with her connections, was able to get the drug charges thrown out. She had been through a lot with Rico Grady, known in the streets as Goo. But Candy wasn't rushing into a marriage because Goo had been known to entertain other hoes in the past, and she wasn't built to deal with his foolishness.

"Fuck Mona... and you the *only* one that can handle Goo."

"You been around Malik too long," Candy laughed and Micah joined in.

"I got some pizza and wings from *Home Run*. Let's eat before it gets cold."

Candy followed her girl to the kitchen, and they fixed their plates. They caught up and talked shit for almost three hours. Candy told Micah about her cousin Ebony that would coming to live with her soon to go to school and caught her up with her family back home. Candy was doing a good deed that she prayed wouldn't backfire. RJ was knocked out, so Candy decided to head on home. She knew that Goo and Malik's asses were going to be out damn near all night, and she wasn't about to wait up on him. After hugging Micah goodnight, Candy headed back home.

The next morning, she woke up to RJ pulling her hair, and she knew damn well that he wasn't in the bed with her when she went to sleep. Saturday was the only day of the week that she really got a chance to sleep in, but it appeared that RJ wasn't going for that.

"You don't want mama to sleep?" she rolled over and tickled him.

"Where your big head daddy go?" Candy got up and went to the bathroom.

After she washed her face and brushed her teeth real quick, Candy picked up RJ and headed to kitchen so that she could fix some breakfast. When she looked at the clock, she noticed that it was almost ten, so she really did get to sleep in. Candy heard the front door open as she walked down the hall and met with Goo with *IHOP* bags when she made it to the living room.

"Good morning. I can't believe you got up this early after being out all night," she kissed Goo.

"You know I'm like Jeezy... sleep when I die," he smacked her on the ass.

Candy placed RJ in his high chair and began pulling the plates out of the bags. Goo had got her the stuffed French toast meal and she couldn't wait to dig in, but she cut up some small pieces first. RJ didn't eat table foods all the time, but ever since Goo started giving him small bites, that was pretty much all he wanted. Candy still gave him baby food in the jar and mixed table foods up along the way. He was only eight months and looked like he was about eighteen months.

"Did you and Malik stay outta trouble last night?"

"When do I ever get in trouble?" Goo smirked.

"Still full of shit... what you got planned for the day?"

"Spending the day wit' y'all. What you wanna do?"

Candy cocked her head to the side. She felt like Goo had done some shit to be so nice, but she wasn't going to sweat it. They finished eating and then Candy got up and threw all of the trash away. Goo played with RJ when she finished, and she went to the living room and turned the TV on. She told him that they could decide on where to go in a couple of hours. It didn't matter to her, just spending time with her little family warmed her heart.

*"**Breaking News**... a shootout at a local strip club, Structure, left several wounded and one possible fatality. The cameras in the facility weren't working, so if anyone has any information, please contact the Chicago Police Department at..."*

"Ain't that's where y'all went? Why you didn't say nothing?"

"Huh?"

"Huh my ass... if there's anything I need to know, you better tell me now!" Candy fussed.

When Goo sat down, she knew that it was about to be some shit, so she braced herself for whatever story he was about to tell.

Chapter 3

Ever since his mom's funeral, Mark had been traveling back and forth from New York to

Chicago. He vowed to be there for his sisters and his dad no matter what. He had missed out on so much in a short period of time and told himself that he couldn't be away any longer. It was time for him to move back home for good. Mark boarded the plane at LaGuardia Airport and had a mixture of emotions. He knew that he could go back at any given time, but New York would *never* be home. Tasha had kept him company, and she had come through in the clutch by helping them to find Micah when she went missing, and for that, Mark would forever be grateful. He allowed her to take up the lease on his condo in New York to continue her fresh start. Since she had whooped Aiesha's ass, Mark figured that she shouldn't have any other problems.

An hour and twenty minutes later, the plane landed at Chicago O'Hare International Airport. Since Mark had shipped his belongings to his parents' house, he didn't have to wait on any luggage, so he clicked the Uber app and requested a car. It was Sunday afternoon and not a typical work day for the family, so Mark figured everyone should be at home. The Uber arrived pretty much immediately and dropped him off at his parents' house in Hyde Park a little while later. He got out and rang the doorbell. He hadn't told anyone that he was coming, but they should have put two and two together when his boxes arrived the day before.

"Marrrkkk!! Heeyyy brother!!!" Micah sang, and he was happy to see that she was there visiting.

"Hey Mikey! I'm so glad to see you," he picked her up and gave her a bear hug.

"They didn't tell me you were coming."

"I didn't tell them, but *my shit* is here somewhere, so somebody knows. Mesha and daddy here?"

"Yep... Mesha just finished cooking and daddy's in the living room. Come on, it's cold out here."

Mark followed his sister into the house and the aroma of food hit his nostrils instantly. He walked towards the kitchen and tried to sneak up on Mesha, but she turned and saw him, causing the biggest smile to form on her face.

"I knew you were coming, but I didn't know it would be so soon… you're right on time. I just got done cooking," Mesha said after Mark gave her a hug.

Just as Mark was about to ask where his dad was, he heard his booming voice and turned around and locked eyes with him.

"What's up pops?" Mark gave him a dap and a one-armed hug.

"Good to see you, son. How long you here for?"

"I'm back for good."

"Well that's good news… you just gotta…"

"I know pops. Everything gon' be straight."

About five minutes later, the four of them sat down at the table and ate the delicious meal that Mesha had prepared. Mark couldn't help but to wish that his mom was still there, but he quickly diverted his thoughts to business so that he wouldn't get sad. He had a business partner that was flying in the next day. He had already told Malik about Kash, but they would all get a feel of one another soon, including Goo. Mark knew how both of them were about trust and letting people in, but he had confidence that everything would work out just as he had it mapped out. Kash had been there with him in New York from the very beginning.

The next day, Mark got up early and went and handled some business. He knew that he was more than welcome to live at home, and his dad had made it known that he wanted him there. However, Mark was so used to his own space, and he didn't know how that would work. After he ate breakfast, he went and looked at a few condos that piqued his interest when he looked online. Even though Mark had been gone for a few years, he was still familiar with Chicago and the areas, making his search easier. He wasn't going to rush and get a place, but he still needed to be on the lookout.

Mark was scheduled to meet with Malik and Goo at two o'clock, and that time was quickly approaching, so he headed out to the spot. He stopped by *Burger King* and grabbed a whopper with cheese meal with a Coke and smashed it on the way while listening to some old school Kanye, back before he got with Kim and went crazy.

"Like we always do at this time

I go for mine, I got to shine

Now throw your hands up in the sky

I g-go for mine, I got to shine

Now throw your hands up in the sky

Ima get on this TV mama, Ima

Ima put shit down

Hey, hey, hey, hey, hey

Hey, I'm good!"

About twenty minutes later, Mark pulled up to his location and parked. Malik's car was already there, just as he expected. When it came down to business, his brother in-law was the man. Mark put his jacket on, got out, and headed inside. As soon as he made it to the door, he heard tires screeching and turned around and locked eyes with Goo's crazy ass. That nigga was definitely the clown of the crew, but just like Malik, he wouldn't hesitate to take a nigga out if the opportunity presented itself.

"What up bruh?" Mark greeted Malik when he walked in.

"Same ol', same ol'… you know how it go."

"Y'all niggaz tryna start without me?" Goo made his way in.

"We just speaking nigga, chill out," Malik laughed at him.

Malik started off by talking about the shipments and how he was about to change shit around surrounding the timings and locations of the drop-offs. Mark knew from experience that he was making a wise decision because niggas were always lurking and looking for a come up. When you switched shit up, it threw everything off. With the amount money that they made, it would only be a matter of time before someone else tried them.

"So with that being said, Mark I think yo new homie is coming at the perfect time," Malik commented.

"Kash already in. I figured you would wanna meet and get a vibe first," Mark replied.

"I trust yo judgment, plus I made some calls in New York and was told that Kash *is* that nigga. We need that on the team after the shit Mo pulled... and like I said, *I trust you.*"

"So what time this nigga gon' be here though? What time you tell him?" Goo chimed in.

"We had business to discuss first and I..."

Before Mark could finish his sentence, his phone rang.

"What up Kash? Yeah, come on in," Mark said and hung up.

A few moments later, the door opened and Mark's homie walked in.

"What the fuck... you brought a bi..."

"Nigga, if *you* call *me a bitch*, Ima shoot yo ass before you have time to blink," Kash cut Goo off and the room fell silent.

Chapter 4

Ebony sat in the front seat of her mother's red Dodge Charger with her arms folded, staring out of the window. It was a three-and-a-half-hour drive from Michigan to Chicago. That was a ride that they took often in the summer, but Ebony wasn't too thrilled about the current visit.

"I don't care about you over there pouting. All of this is *your* fault," Ebony's mother Patricia said from the driver's seat.

"*My fault?* It's *my* fault that I want to grow up, but you won't let me," Ebony replied.

"Girl, you better watch yo tone, and it's not the growing up part I have a problem with. It's the choices you make in life that I do."

"*Choices?* Mom, I've done everything you asked of me. I got good grades, stayed out of trouble, and graduated high school, yet you are forcing college on me," Ebony stated as tears began to cloud her vision.

"*Forcing?* Eb that is because college is *not an option* in this family, *it is mandatory*. You lied and told us that you filled out applications and just having bad luck. I knew that couldn't have been the case because you are a straight A student. Your father and I love you but moving to Chicago and staying with Candy is what's best for you?"

"And how you figure?" Ebony blurted out.

"Candy has her shit together. You need to surround yourself with individuals like her. Y'all not that far apart in age, and she's an attorney. I know not only will she look out for you, but she'll give you the push that you need," Mrs. Bell looked over at her only child and stated.

Ebony didn't bother to respond because it was like beating a dead horse, and she knew her mother wouldn't see things her way. College was cool, but it wasn't for her. Yeah, she had the drive and smarts to be anything in this world; it's just that… she didn't want to. Her dreams and her mother's dreams didn't match and that was the biggest problem.

Ebony placed her headphones in her ear and tuned her mother out for the rest of the ride. The sounds of Beyoncé's station on *Pandora* soothed her into a much-needed nap. When she woke up, they were pulling into a driveway of a nice two-story brick house.

"You up? Let's get the bags out of the trunk," Her mom said, placing the car in park.

Ebony let out a long sigh before unbuckling her seatbelt and following her mom's lead. The both of them grabbed the suitcases out of the trunk and headed up the stairs to Candy's home. Mrs. Bell rang the doorbell, and a few seconds later, the doors swung up. Candy stood in the doorway with a huge smile plastered across her face.

"Auntttiiieeee!" Candy squealed, hugging her favorite aunt.

"You look amazing! You can't tell that you even had a baby. Speaking of baby, where is little RJ?" Mrs. Bell asked, looking around for the toddler.

"Oh, he went to the barbershop with his dad. They should be back in a little while. Come on in," Candy replied.

"Hey Ebony, how you doing?" Candy asked, grabbing her aunt's coat to hang up.

"I been good Diamond!" Ebony replied.

Candy busted out in laughter while her aunt looked on in confusion.

"Who is Diamond?" she asked.

"Diamond off *"The Player's Club."* Her name is Ebony, I'm her cousin, and she's coming to live with me…. Ohhhh never mind auntie," Candy giggled, waving her off.

Ebony couldn't help but laugh that time herself. She always thought that Candy was uptight. She prayed like hell she was wrong or it was going to be a *long* six months.

"So how far is the school from here?" Mrs. Bell asked, taking a seat on the couch.

"Oh, *Northwestern* is like 20 minutes away. Ebony can drive my Benz whenever she needs it, and I'll take my Porsche truck," Candy replied, winking her eye at Ebony who smiled.

Candy whipped up a quick meal that consisted of chicken wings and fries. The ladies sat around and talked until it was time for Mrs. Bell to get back on the road.

"Now Candy, you're my sister's child, so I know you gon' look out for my baby," she said, hugging Candy and then doing the same with Ebony.

"Of course, I got you. She'll be in medical school before you know it," Candy assured her.

"That's what I like to hear."

Mrs. Bell finally left, leaving the girls alone.

"Ok girl, let me show you your room. You can have anything in this house. You are *not* a guest at this point, you live here. If you need anything, just let me know," Candy explained to her younger cousin.

"Cool. Aye Candy, your place is beautiful," Ebony said, admiring her home.

"Thank you, I try to keep it clean, but with an almost one-year-old, it's not the easiest."

"I bet! I can't wait to meet RJ. I seen some pictures at your mom's house. He is so handsome."

"Thank you, girl, and he will be crawling through here any minute now. Make yourself at home while I go see what we gon' eat for dinner," Candy said, leaving Ebony alone.

Ebony flopped down on the king size bed, pulling her vibrating phone out of her bra.

"Yo!" she answered on like the third ring.

"*Me and you will never part... la te da da*"

Ebony sat up and laughed so hard, she started choking. Her best friend Megan called singing the song from *The Color Purple* loudly in her ears.

"Bitch you so stupid. What up?" Ebony said once she gathered her composure.

"I still can't believe you left me," Megan whined.

"It wasn't like I had a choice."

"You grown as *fuck*! You definitely had a choice."

"Tell *that shit* to my momma. I can't stand her ass," Ebony fumed, folding her arms across her chest.

"Yeah. Yeah. Yeah. So how is *Ms. Attorney at Law*? Megan questioned.

"She good. Bougie as expected, but I guess she's cool," Ebony shrugged.

"Yeah, I bet. I bet her nigga is as uptight as her. Probably some old *khaki pants wearing* ass lame." Megan stated.

"Well I haven't met him yet, his out…. wait… as a matter of fact, I think he just came in."

Ebony stood to her feet and walked to the bedroom door and looked out.

"Oh my God bitch!" she whispered into the phone.

"What? What? What?" Megan panicked.

"This motherfucker is *fine!*"

"Fine as in *Carlton Banks* fine or fine as in *Future* fine?" Megan quizzed.

"Fine as in *Future* fine. This nigga tall, skinny with dreads, and by looking at the Timbs and Gucci shirt, he *ain't* no lame."

"Swear to God!" Megan screamed.

"I swear, maybe *Miss Perfect* not so perfect at all..." Ebony smirked.

Chapter 5

"Here you go. Get yo bad ass son," Goo walked in and yelled, tossing RJ to his mother.

"Boy don't be throwing my baby. What's wrong with you?" Candy asked as she tickled the almost one-year-old.

"That nigga there don't know how to stop playing," Goo said, walking into the kitchen and looking in the refrigerator.

"Well baby, he's a kid sooooooo..." Candy stated, shrugging her shoulders.

"Fuck all that. He need some Benadryl or something. We in the barbershop and he wanna crawl every got damn where. Won't be still for *shit*," Goo vented.

"And who coat is this?" He continued, walking passed the chair that contained Ebony's white North Face.

"Ohhh, my cousin Ebony is here. Remember I told you she was coming?"

"Yeah... what you cooking tho?" Goo asked.

"I have the slightest idea, but we need to talk," Candy's voice changed to a serious tone.

Goo looked at her suspiciously as he took a bite from the oatmeal cream pie he pulled from the cabinet.

"Look, it wasn't me," he joked, walking over to where she was and pulling her into a hug.

"Rico, I'm serious. Let me put RJ in his bed, and I'll be back."

Goo gave her a kiss on the lips before releasing his grip. He knew that anytime a woman said *she needed to talk*, it was never about anything good. He walked over to the couch, grabbed the remote, and flipped through the channels until she came back in the room. Candy returned about five minutes later and sat next to him.

"What's up baby?" he asked, his eyes never shifting from the TV.

"We never really dug deep into the situation after you got out of jail, but I think now is the time," she replied.

"Dug into what situation?" he asked with a raised eyebrow.

"You and this street shit."

"OK, what about it?" he questioned.

"What the fuck you gon' do? I know you don't expect this shit to last forever, and what about me and your son?" she asked.

Goo grabbed the remote control that was now on the side of him and muted the TV before turning to Candy.

"Baby, *I'm* a street nigga. I don't know what else to tell you. No, I don't stand on corners, but these are my streets. What do you want me to do?" he questioned.

"I want you to *stop*. Look at me! *I'm* a fucking lawyer, how that look?"

"It looks like I'll have all the free legal advice if I need it."

"RICO I'M SERIOUS!" the volume of her voice increased.

"Candy, I love the fuck outta you. You and RJ are *my everything*, but *this* is me. I'm not trying to retire doing this shit... but look around. We good. I'm twenty-five living the life niggaz more than half my age ain't living."

"At what cost though? I ain't trying to explain to our son that his daddy *never* coming home," Candy replied.

"And you'll *never* have to tell him no shit like that. Listen to me, I swear to God on my OG, after we done with this upcoming move, I'll slow down, possibly even stopping, but I gotta handle this first. Mark back in Chicago, and he brought his partner Kash with him. We about to make some moves," he explained.

Speaking on the *Kash* situation, he needed to call Mark and holler at him about it. He spoke highly of his homie, but imagine the shock on his and Malik's face when they found out that his homie was *a bitch*. Goo didn't have a problem with women working *for* him. It was the working *alongside* him that he didn't like. Goo felt as if women worked off emotions, and there was no time for that bullshit in the drug game. His point was proven when the bitch pulled a gun on him for calling her *a bitch*. Mark was going to be responsible for shorty if she turned out to be a problem. His crew was good with them three. Mark just had to fuck things up.

"Whatever Goo," Candy said, rolling her eyes.

It was clear that she wasn't done with the conversation, but decided to cut it short because she heard Ebony's bedroom door open. Goo eyes shifted to the hallway where they landed on a short thick chick. Ebony was about 5'2 with a nice set of curves. She wore her hair in a short cut that stopped a little bit above her ears. Just looking at her in the face, you could tell she was young. Her face screamed youthfulness, but her eyes told a different story.

"Ebony, this is my boyfriend Goo, Goo this is my cousin Ebony," Candy stood to her feet, introducing the two.

"Nice to meet you Goo," Ebony replied with a friendly smile.

"Same to you shorty," Goo replied with a head nod before unmuting the TV and getting back to the game.

He wasn't too thrilled about Candy having someone living with her, but technically, he was living with her too since Mona vandalized the crib they had together. At first, he was going to just chill there, but now, he was seriously thinking about grabbing a condo or something quick.

"Ima order a pizza. Y'all want that?" Goo heard Candy yell from the kitchen.

"Yeah that's cool. I'm about to take a shower, I'll be back," Goo announced before heading upstairs to the bathroom.

He peeked inside to check on his son, who was sleeping peacefully before doing so. Once inside the bathroom, Goo cut the hot water on and hopped in. He washed up a few times before stepping out and drying off. He then went inside the room and threw on some basketball shorts and a wife-beater. He placed his phone on the charger before he got in the shower. Noticing that he had a little juice now, he unplugged it and jumped in the bed. Goo checked the apps on his phone, including ESPN and CNN. He wasn't into social media;

therefore, all the apps he had dealt with news in some form or fashion. After scrolling through and reading, the doorbell rang and seconds later, Candy called out for him to come down and eat. Goo snatched up his phone and headed downstairs where he found Ebony sitting at the counter while Candy set out the plates. Goo took a seat across from her just as Candy sat about five slices of sausage and pepperoni pizza, along with a few hot wings on his plate as well. After she was done, she took a seat next to her cousin and dug in.

"So Ebony, are you excited about starting school?" Candy asked, breaking the silence in the kitchen.

"Honestly cousin, not really. I don't think you have to go to college to be successful," Ebony replied.

"Smart girl," Goo slid in, never looking up at them.

"Well, although that is true, a lot comes with having a college degree," Candy replied.

"Yeah student loans," Ebony stated, causing Goo to chuckle a little bit.

"What the fuck you laughing at?" Candy cut her eyes at him and asked.

"Nothing man. Talk to your cousin," Goo laughed as he continued to stuff his face.

"Don't get me wrong, college is cool and all, but some of us are not cut out for that shit," Ebony stated.

"Like, would y'all *force* college on RJ if he didn't want to go?" she continued.

"*Yes*," Candy blurted out followed by Goo yelling "*NO!*"

Candy looked over at Goo and gave him a look, but it didn't faze him. He was a firm believer that college didn't determine whether you would be successful or not, and Candy wasn't going to change that.

"Cuzn, I see why you say yes, that's because you are a successful attorney. Goo, if you don't mind me asking, what is it you do for a living?" Ebony inquired.

"I own a few businesses, including a car wash, and I'm part owner of a night club," he boasted.

"See! My point proven," Ebony rejoiced.

"His situation is different," a frustrated Candy stated.

"And how is that?" Ebony questioned, looking back and forth at the both of them.

"Girl, eat yo food, you going to college, end of story!" Candy replied, dismissing Ebony's question.

Chapter 6

To say that Candy was frustrated with Goo would have been an understatement. She was righteously pissed. Candy loved Goo with all of her heart, but she really had some decisions to make about life for her and her son. The thought of Goo getting caught up and going to jail or even worse, him dying wasn't something that she could sit back and settle for. Him talking down about college in front of Ebony added to her frustrations that much more. Candy knew that she wasn't perfect, but she had worked too damn hard to allow anyone to set her back. Now that she had a son, it meant that she had to grind one hundred times harder. Raising a black man was now one of the hardest things to do. The way police officers were shooting innocent young black men without a care in the world had put fear in Candy's heart, and her son wasn't even one. She wished that he could stay a baby forever but that wasn't possible. She knew that she had to do any and everything possible to protect him and that would be with or without Goo by her side. The ringing of Candy's office phone pulled her from her thoughts.

"Hey Krystal," she answered once she looked and saw that it was her secretary calling.

"Hey boss lady. Your eleven o'clock has agreed to reschedule, and you're clear until two o'clock."

"Thank you so much Krystal. I appreciate it. Once I return from helping my cousin, you'll be free to go."

"It's no problem. I'm just doing my job."

"And you do it so well, but I'm forcing you to leave when I get back," Candy smiled and hung up.

Candy closed her MacBook Pro, grabbed her phone and purse, and then headed out. It was a little after ten, and Candy was headed to pick Ebony up and take her to orientation. She had initially told her that she could drive the extra vehicle, but she had made a mistake and grabbed both sets of keys. She made her way back to her place, called Ebony, and the look on her face when she walked out of the door let Candy know that she wasn't too thrilled about attending college. Candy silently wondered if she had made a mistake by agreeing to let her cousin live with her because she didn't have time to be monitoring Ebony's every move and making sure that she was going to class. Her aunt made it seem like she was excited since she was attending school in Chicago, but according to conversation they had the other day, Ebony wasn't really feeling school at all.

"You ain't gotta look so sad," Candy said when Ebony got into the car.

"I really just don't know if college is for me, cousin. I see how successful you are, but I'm not you, and I feel like my mama forcing me to be like you," Ebony sighed.

Candy backed out of the driveway and made her way towards Northwestern. She had to think before speaking because she didn't want to say the wrong thing. It was true that school wasn't for everyone, but you had to have some kind of plan to make it in the world. She prayed that her little cousin wasn't one of those people that felt like the world owed her shit.

"So what is it that you wanna do in life?" Candy finally inquired.

"You don't really want the answer to that... but I can tell you I wouldn't need school."

She saw Ebony smirk out of the corner of her eye and sighed.

"How about this... just give it a try. I can tell you that it'll be boring at first, but once you get into your core classes, it'll be interesting. With the way the world is setup, a Bachelor's degree is damn near equivalent to a high school diploma," Candy explained.

"I don't need a degree to be like Goo, do I?"

"Leave Goo outta this and forget about what he said," Candy rolled her eyes.

She could see that playing nice to her cousin wasn't going to go over too well and that comment made her mad at Goo all over again. About twenty minutes later, Candy turned onto Clark Street. The campus of Northwestern was in view, and it was something beautiful.

"You wanna stay on campus if a dorm becomes available?" Candy asked as she parked her Benz.

"Naahhh… ion really like people in my space like that. Ima test out the commuting thing first and see how I like it," Ebony replied.

This little chick is something serious, Candy thought to herself as she got out of the car. They made their way to the Admissions building and signed in. Ebony seemed to perk up when she saw a couple of cute fine ass guys.

"I might like Chicago after all," Ebony smiled.

"They are fine," Candy noted.

"Whaatttt… you really surprising me big cousin! First you got a thug ass nigga and you still checking out other dudes."

"Ebony, let's not get it twisted. I'm a professional, but I'm still me. Don't think thug ass niggaz is where it's at all the time either. That shit comes wit' a headache. Don't look at my life and think shit is sweet. It's hard as hell and I hope you make better choices," Candy tried to school her.

"Yeah yeah yeah… let's go find these buildings, so I won't be stuck looking stupid tomorrow," Ebony shrugged her off.

Since Ebony was a week late registering, there wasn't a crowd and she was able to handle her business quickly. They stayed on campus about an hour and then left and headed to get something to eat. Candy still had a couple of hours to spare and decided that she would take her cousin to get some chicken from *Uncle Remus*. It had been a minute since Candy had some and the thought of some wings and fries made her stomach growl. Candy called and placed an order so that it would be ready when they got there. As soon as she hung up, her phone rang and she looked down and saw her girl calling.

"Hey boo… what's goin' on?" Candy answered.

"Shit… just 'bout to leave the funeral home and grab some lunch. You eating out today or staying in?"

"I just placed an order at *Uncle Remus* then Ima go back to the house to eat before I go back to the office. You want something from there?"

"Yeah Ima call and add to your order, and I'll meet you at your place."

Fifteen minutes later, Candy pulled up and it was packed as fuck, just as she expected. She saw a couple of dudes off to side and prayed that her order was ready because it was possible for anyone to start shooting at any given moment. Candy walked in and stood in line for about five minutes. Thankfully, her food was ready and she was out of there. An eerie feeling came over Candy, so she picked up her pace and hopped back in her truck. As soon as she got in, gun shots rang out, and she hurriedly threw her car in gear and got the hell out of dodge.

"Got damn... you gon' break my neck," Ebony squealed.

"You better hold on, so I can get the fuck outta here," Candy fussed as she whipped out of the parking lot.

"I knew them niggaz was up to no good over there. Shoulda just took an L and left right away."

It was sad that being around gunshots was the norm in Chicago. That incident right there let Candy know that it really might be time for her to part ways with the city. She didn't want her son to grow up in that bullshit. The question was, would Goo ever leave or would she be forced to take her son and leave on her own when the timing was right?

Chapter 7

The meeting the other day with the guys and Kash had gone well, at least it did after the initial incident with Kash and Goo. Mark knew that she was a hot head, but she was one that demanded respect just like them, and that was why he knew that she would be a good fit. He met Kash two months after he arrived in New York, and she had been down with him ever since. Even though she was fine as fuck, they had never crossed those lines. Mark knew that he would eventually get him a place, but he wasn't really pressed for one. He planned on spending the day helping Kash find a place and getting settled in. She was staying at the Marriott, and it was around ten o'clock when he pulled into the parking lot and called her to let her know that he was downstairs.

Mark's phone chimed, and he clicked the message icon and noticed that it was Aiesha. Even though he had left New York and told her the real deal, she still didn't stop reaching out to him. Honestly, he would never be able to look at her the same because of the way that she had acted during one of his most vulnerable times. He read the texts and once again ignored them. He had his read receipts on, so she knew that he saw them. If she got the hint, cool; if not, that was fine by him too because he was over her.

"Get out the phone and unlock the door nigga," Kash hollered and interrupted his thoughts.

"Damn you made it down here fast as fuck," Mark said when she got in.

"Oh I meant to tell you they had a first floor room available right before I got the key and I took it. Right by the exit."

"Aight... let's go find you somewhere to stay. You been out anywhere in my city yet?"

"Nigga this ain't yo city. It's mine," Kash laughed.

"You left when you was still a toddler, so ain't shit about you that says Chicago," he jested.

"I was born at *RUSH!* That means I'm Chicago. Next subject."

"You lucky Goo didn't pop yo ass the other day. Why you pull a gun on the homie?"

"Trust me, I knew he wasn't 'bout to shoot me. He was too caught off guard, so I took advantage of the situation, plus let them know I ain't one to be slept on," Kash shrugged.

"I don't know what Ima do wit' yo ass," Mark chuckled.

"Love me like you been doing," Kash replied and then pulled her phone out of her pocket.

Mark maneuvered through the streets of his city and made his way to Willow Lake Apartments out in the suburbs. He saw that they had a vacancy when he looked online, and he hoped that Kash would like the place because it was in a nice neighborhood. It was actually one that he might move in, but he wanted to give her first choice. He noticed the look on her face when they pulled up, and it seemed as if she was pleased with the surroundings.

"You thought I was 'bout to take you to a fucked up neighborhood huh? When you start doubting me?" he teased.

"You know you be slipping sometimes, so I gotta stay on you," Kash joked.

Mark park in front of the leasing office and killed the engine. He put his coat on and got out. The manager greeted them as soon as they walked in, and Mark was pleased about that. His parents had always taught him the value of respect and instilled in all of them to never spend money in a place that they felt disrespected. The white lady offered them a drink, but they declined before following her lead as she led them to a model apartment.

"This is a nice neighborhood and plenty of couples love it here because of the quietness, so I'm sure you two lovebirds will fit right in," she expressed.

Mark and Kash busted out laughing simultaneously, and it caused the woman to stop in her tracks.

"Miss, we are *NOT* a couple. He's like my brother," Kash finally spoke after she got her laughter in check.

"Damn ma… it's like that? You coulda let the lady think we was a couple," Mark told Kash.

"Yo ass was laughing too," she rolled her eyes.

"I'm so sorry... I just... I thought... never mind. I'm sorry. Please forgive me," the woman uttered.

"It's cool. She ain't ready for a man like me," Mark hinted.

The woman led them into the apartment, and both of them were impressed with the layout. Mark asked when Kash would be able to move in if she decided on it, and they were told that there were two apartments available. She showed them a layout of the entire complex once they made it back to the office. Kash loved the place and decided that she would take the vacancy in building C and Mark went ahead and signed for building G. He paid security deposits and first and last month rent for both of their places.

"You know I can pay for my own shit right?" Kash said after they were done and back in the car.

"How often do you pay for shit when you wit' me?"

"Exactly... so chill out," Mark said after she didn't answer his question.

Mark always looked out for Kash, and he planned on keeping it that way no matter what. He knew that she didn't let many people close to her because of shit that she had gone through in the past and he understood. Both of her parents died in a house fire when she was only five years old. That was the reason she left Chicago. Kash expressed to him how she overheard her aunt saying that her parents were killed, but no one ever found out exactly who was responsible for their deaths. He knew that Kash wanted answers. It didn't matter that it had been years. When her aunt died three years ago, she was once again left alone. She had often spoke on moving back to Chicago, and when the opportunity presented itself, Mark offered her a job with the home team and she accepted.

"Ima let you meet my sisters, and they can help you wit' that decorating shit. You know I ain't wit' all that."

"That's cool," Kash replied, and Mark was surprised that she didn't put up a fuss.

After they grabbed something to eat, Mark headed to the dealership and surprised Kash with a silver Audi A8. He had been stacking money for a long ass time, and he really wanted her to be in a happy space since she was in Chicago, where the root of her problems started.

"You tryna turn me into a lil weak bitch I see... *thank you* Mark. I owe you," Kash sincerely told him.

"Everything that I've told you has been real... always will be. I got you."

When they were finishing up, Malik called Mark and told him to meet up with him ASAP. He told Kash that he would get up with her later and dipped out to see what the urgency was in his brother in-law's voice.

Chapter 8

It was one thing hearing about all the shootings and killings on the news, but being in an actual shootout was something that Ebony did not prepare herself for. She thought about calling her mom and exaggerating the story a little bit. Maybe if she told her that she was grazed by a bullet, then she would come back and get her. But knowing her mom, she'd chuck it up to her being at the wrong place at the wrong time and still make her go to class.

"I sure do hope this chicken is worth damn near dying," Ebony stated as they pulled in Candy's garage.

"The chicken cool; it's the mild sauce that's worth it. Wait until you taste it," Candy replied, hitting the button to let the doors down.

"I'll be the judge of that," Ebony shrugged as she walked behind Candy into her home.

The two of them entered into the kitchen and placed the greasy bags on the counter before washing their hands.

"Let me go grab my charger, I'll be back. Your food is in that bag right there," Candy said, pointing to the bag farthest left.

Without a response, Ebony rambled through the bag and was pulling out her food when the doorbell rang.

"I'm on the toilet. Can you get that?" Candy yelled from upstairs.

Ebony sat her food down and headed to the door.

"Who is it?" she asked.

"Micah," a voice from the other side could be heard saying.

Ebony remembered Candy saying something about her friend coming over to join them, so she opened the door.

"You must be Ebony, nice to meet you," Micah said, extending her hand for a handshake.

"Yup! Candy will be right down. Come on in," Ebony replied, closing the door behind her.

Micah and Ebony both went into the kitchen. As soon as they took a seat, Candy joined them.

"Hey girl!" Candy smiled, greeting her friend.

"Hey, where's my baby?" Micah looked around and asked.

"Oh, he's at daycare. Hopefully Goo picks him up cause Lord knows I don't feel like it," she replied, taking a seat and grabbing a fry out of the bag.

"That fool was just over our house," Micah said, shaking her head.

"I don't know how you deal with him?" she continued.

"Y'all tripping. Goo cool as fuck," Ebony added in, digging into her chicken breast.

"He aight," Candy laughed while Micah eyed Ebony, who caught the glimpse.

"Anyway. What clubs popping? If I'm going to be stuck in this cold, dangerous ass city, I might as well have some fun," Ebony stated as she twerked in her seat.

"How about you not even twenty-one yet?" Candy replied, shutting down her little cousin hopes.

"And there's more to my city than cold weather and bullets," Micah added in.

"Yeah like what?" Ebony asked, rolling her eyes.

"Like LIFE! Maybe you should focus on school and then the partying later," Micah replied.

"Who the fuck are you? *My momma?*" Ebony snapped.

"*No,* but I'm one of those Chicago bitches who will punch you in yo shit if you disrespect me again," Micah snapped back.

"HOLD UP! HOLD UP! HOLD UP! The both of y'all need to chill. Ebony, she's right, focus on school, get your bread up, and then worry about partying," Candy said, defusing the situation.

"I get that cousin, all I'm saying is, I need to do shit other than study," a more calmer Ebony replied but not before rolling her eyes at Micah.

"Speaking of studying, you ready for graduation in a few months?" Candy turned to Micah and asked.

"As a matter of fact, I am. I can't wait to get this degree. Lord knows it has been a journey," Micah beamed at the thought of receiving her Bachelor's Degree in May.

"I know friend and you know I'm going to be front row, cheering you on."

The two friends talked about a few more things while Ebony listened on. She had made up her mind about Micah: she didn't like her at all. She seemed to be one of those bitches who didn't mind their own business. Ebony wasn't a fighter, but she wasn't a punk either. She ran across bitches like Micah all the time back in Michigan. She had a feeling that Candy's little bitch ass friend was gon' have to see her. In due time.

"Aye Ebony! I was just telling Micah about how stressed I am, and I know you must be too. I was thinking about a mini-shopping spree, on me," Candy said, jolting Ebony out of her thoughts.

"Shopping spree, I'm down. I have my daddy's credit card, so I'm good," she replied.

"Ohhhh isn't someone spoiled?" Micah and Candy laughed.

Just as Ebony was about to give the both of them a piece of her mind, the front door opened and Goo, along with the finest man Ebony had ever laid eyes on, entered.

"Speaking of the devil, we were just talking about you," Candy said to Goo, who walked over and gave her a kiss.

"Y'all motherfuckers went to *Uncle Remus* and ain't grab me nothing?" Goo barked, taking two pieces of chicken out of Candy's plate.

"That is some petty shit," Malik added in, taking a seat next to Micah.

"Malik this is my cousin Ebony, Ebony this is Malik," Candy introduced, making sure everyone was acquainted.

"Heyyyyy Malik," Ebony sang, followed by a flirty wave.

"Slow yo road kid, this is *MY* husband," Micah snapped.

Ebony heard her loud and clear, but it didn't matter to her none. Sure, Micah was cute, but Ebony felt as if she didn't hold a candle to her. Although she hated staying in Chicago, *Mr. Malik* had just what it took to make her call the Windy City home.

Chapter 9

"Dirty soda in a styrofoam
Spend a day to get my mind blown
Dress it up and go to NASA
200 miles on the dash
Gotta roll a pound up and gas it
Switching lanes in a Grand Rapid
We the ones that kept it cool with all these niggas till these niggas
start acting
Shoot a nigga like a film in a movie, nigga, gon' let 'em have it
We ballin' like the March Madness
All these cops shooting niggas, tragic
I'm the one that's living lavish
Like I'm playing for the Mavericks
I didn't wanna fuck that bitch, the molly made me fuck her even though
she average
Dirty muddy in my cup."

Goo's head bobbed up and down as he cruised the North Lawndale area on the Westside of Chicago, listening to his favorite Future's song, *March Madness*. He looked around and the fresh snow on the ground made him miss summer. Summertime in the Chi was always lit, but with the way shit was set up, niggaz was lucky to see another summer. The weather was in the low thirties, which was considered decent in February. Goo was pretty much free, so he figured he'd make some plans with Candy. It had been a minute since they been out together. With the baby, her career, and the shit Goo had going on, the only time they seemed to see each other was in passing.

Goo reached into the cup holder to grab his phone when it started ringing in his hand. He looked at the screen, noticing it was one of his workers reaching out. Goo answered the call and headed to meet them at their crib to pick up some bread. Goo took Homan all the way to Chicago Ave where he made a right, heading towards Hamlin. When he pulled up front, he hopped out and went inside the three-flat building. The front door was already opened, so he took the stairs to the second floor, where he knocked hard on the door. He checked his phone while he waited for Tammy to answer. When she finally opened it, she stood there wearing a pair of pink laced boy shorts and a white baby-tee. Goo licked his lips as he looked her up and down.

"You gon' stand there with yo dick hard or you gon' come in and get this bread nigga?" she asked, turning away and walking back inside before he could answer.

Goo watched her ass shake as she made her way further into the small apartment.

"That lame ass nigga gone?" he asked, taking a seat on the gray sectional.

"Would I let you in here if he wasn't?" she replied, twisting her head to the side.

"Low key you would," he laughed.

Goo watched Tammy walk out the room and return back with a duffle bag full of money. She placed the bag on the coffee table before walking over to where Goo was sitting.

"Hold on. I ain't staying," he said as she tried to remove his jacket.

"And why not?" she asked in a flirty tone before straddling him.

"Cuz man, I told you I'm not on this anymore."

"Candy got you whipped now huh?" she whispered, licking his earlobe.

"Keep my bitch name out yo mouth," he replied sternly, lifting her off of him and standing to his feet.

"My bad, but I bet she can't suck yo dick like I can."

Tammy tugged on Goo's jeans, pulling him closer to her before dropping to her knees. She then unbuckled his Gucci belt, pulling his pants down. She reached inside his draws and began to play with his dick. Goo had all intentions on stopping her, but like she said, *Candy can't suck dick like she can.* Tammy was a fool with it. When it came to pleasing Goo, she cut no corners.

"Tammy chill," Goo said, looking down as she placed his dick in her mouth.

Tammy ignored him and went to work on his dick and balls. Goo gave up on trying to stop her and enjoyed the head instead. Tammy placed all nine inches inside her mouth until his dick was practically down her throat. Goo felt himself about to nut, so he closed his eyes and released in her mouth. Tammy looked up at him and smiled, all the while swallowing his kids.

"Now make me feel good," Tammy stood to her feet and began to slide out of her panties.

Goo's dick grew a few inches again, looking at her body. It had been a while since he had some *outside* pussy. Him and Tammy had been fucking around for a few years off and on. Her and her husband worked for Goo and Malik, and whenever ol' buddy wasn't around, Goo broke her off; but as of lately, he stopped. He was trying to do the faithful thing with Candy but the bitches were tempting. Goo literally tried to decide what move to make, but with Tammy playing with his newly hardened dick, she wasn't helping.

Fuck it, I'll start being faithful again tomorrow, Goo said to himself before pulling Tammy closer to him and started playing with her pussy. Just as he was about to bend her over, their front door opened and in walked her husband James.

"WHAT THE FUCK GOING ON IN HERE?!" James yelled as he walked closer to the pair.

Goo looked over at Tammy, who looked like she was on the verge of a heart attack, and laughed.

"Oh my God baby!" she screamed as she fumbled around in search of her panties.

Goo bent down and pulled up his pants, his eyes never leaving James. James looked over at Goo like he wanted to say something, but he knew better.

"Bitch, Ima kill you," James screamed at his wife of seven years.

"Man do that shit when I ain't here," Goo said, grabbing the duffle bag off of the coffee table.

Before he could make it to the door, his cell phone rang. He looked down and Candy's name and picture flashed across. He attempted *to reject* the call but made a mistake and answered it instead.

"What up? I'm in the middle of some shit right now, I'll call you back," was all he said to her before ending the call.

He didn't mean to be so brief, but he had too much shit going on at the moment. Goo left the couple arguing and finally headed to his car. As soon as he got it, his phone rang again. This time it was Timmy, another worker calling. Goo thought about ignoring his call as well but decided to answer instead.

"YO!"

"Aye Boss, we got a problem," he spoke.

"Handle it," Goo instructed.

"Nah, I think this one requires your attention. I'm at the house on Douglas and Central Park."

"On my way," Goo instructed before ending the call.

Goo needed to stop at his crib and drop off the money before heading towards the trap house. There was no way he was going to be caught with that type of cash on him. On the drive there, he thought about what Candy said about getting out the game. If it wasn't one thing, it was another. The street shit was becoming too stressful.

Chapter 10

"Your Honor, the tapes that the prosecutor is speaking of cannot be entered into evidence because my client had no knowledge of being recorded."

"She's right, Attorney Benson… and I'm pretty sure you knew this. Ladies and gentlemen of the jury, please disregard the last few statements that were made by Attorney Benson," Judge Crimson stated before giving Benson a brief but firm stare.

Both attorneys delivered their closing remarks and then the jury was sent to deliberate. Candy excused herself from her client and went to the restroom. She was so happy that it was the last day of the trial and said another silent prayer for a good outcome. Her client was being accused of breeching confidentiality on the job and Medicaid fraud, but Candy had presented evidence that she was framed. It was her first case against a mental health facility, and it was a pretty big one. However, she was very confident because she had put in extra work to prepare and her client had been straight up with her from the very beginning.

Ten minutes later, Candy made her way back to the courtroom and found her client sitting in the same spot, looking nervous.

"Everything is gonna work out," she told her in an attempt to comfort her.

The jury returned and took their seats. They all kept straight faces that Candy couldn't read. She knew that she had worked her ass off on the case and prayed that the sleepless nights and long hours paid off.

"Has the jury reached a verdict?"

"We have your Honor!" the spokesman of the jury stated.

"We find the defendant…. NOT GUILTY!"

Candy smiled and so did her client. The prosecutor and his clients face turned red as hell, and Candy willed herself not to smirk at them. They had done every trick in the book to try and railroad her client on some bogus ass charges, and she was happy they she had people in high places. There were far too many innocent people in jail, and she vowed to do everything possible to prevent anymore from going whenever the opportunity presented itself. She looked at her client, and she had tears in her eyes.

"Thank you so much Ms. Williams. My last attorney told me that I would be paying money back and looking at five years minimum."

Candy wanted to tell her that her last lawyer was probably working with the State, but instead, Candy told her that she was happy that she could help. She also let her know that everything would be expunged and that she was good to go. Once court was officially adjourned, Candy hugged her client one last time, and they walked out together. When they parted ways, Candy hopped into her Benz and made the ten minute drive back to her office. She didn't feel like stopping for lunch, so she placed an order for delivery. It was almost noon and traffic was about to get crazier. She knew the city all too well.

When Candy walked in, she spoke to her assistant, retrieved her messages, and headed to her office. It looked like her assistant wanted to say something else, but she just smiled and spun back around and got to work. Candy walked into her office and her eyes landed on the most beautiful flowers that she had ever seen in her life. The arrangement was breathtaking. Candy smiled at thoughts of Goo. She had been internally battling with their relationship because it seemed that he cared more about the streets than home, but him doing something so spontaneous and beautiful made Candy regret any thoughts that she had for the time being. She pulled her phone out and took a picture and posted it on Snap Chat and shared it to her story.

Candy admired the arrangement again and then picked up her phone to call Goo and tell him thanks. The phone rang a few times and then Goo finally picked up.

"What up," he answered and Candy instantly copped an attitude by his tone, but she looked at the flowers and shrugged it off.

"Hey baby… I was calling to say tha…"

"I'm in the middle of some shit right now. I'll call you back," he cut her off and hung up.

The attitude that she tried to hide instantly reared its ugly head again. What Goo had just done was the very reason she had been in a limbo about their relationship. She began thinking back how absent Goo had been lately. He was a good dad when he was around and lately, that hadn't been too often. It was time for Candy to make some decisions about her life, and she had to do it fast. Candy's office phone rang, and she picked it up. It was her secretary letting her know that her lunch had arrived. A few minutes later, she brought it in with the aroma from *Chipotle* calming Candy's nerves. She had skipped breakfast because she had to go straight to court, and she would be damned if she let Goo's inconsiderate ass fuck up one of her favorite meals.

Candy devoured her steak bowl. It was filled with mixed rice, vegetables, sour cream, and cheese. She opened her mini fridge and grabbed a bottle of water, opened it, and drank half before she sat it down on her desk. After throwing all of the trash away, Candy opened her MacBook and went to *The Children's Place* website. She had few coupons that she needed to use before they expired. Ten minutes later, she had racked up on clothes for RJ. The total was almost three hundred dollars, but after she put her coupon codes in, she purchased everything in her cart for less than two hundred.

After online shopping, Candy got busy on her next case. She had the challenge of defending a black teenager who was in the wrong place at the wrong time. He had great character witnesses, but Candy had a long road ahead of her on that particular case. She did so much research that time got away from her. When she looked at her phone, it was almost four o'clock. She planned on picking RJ up before five, so Candy went ahead and wrapped everything up. Candy closed her MacBook, grabbed her phone and purse, and then prepared to exit. The flowers caught her attention again. The thought of throwing them in the trash crossed her mind, but she went ahead and picked them up and decided to take them home. Leaving them on her desk would have been a constant reminder of how Goo acted when she called, so she decided to take them and show him how beautiful they were and then cuss his ass out.

Candy made it to the daycare a quarter till five. Traffic was a bitch. Some parents didn't pick their kids up until six, but Candy tried to get her soon early when her workload permitted her to do so. The smile on RJ's face when he saw her instantly made her entire day greater.

"Hey mommy's big boy," she smiled.

"Guess what he did today?" the worker said as she walked towards Candy.

"What happened?" Candy asked with a voice full of concern.

She watched as the daycare worker put RJ down, and he took a few steps.

"Oh my God!!" Candy squealed as her son walked the rest of the way to her.

He had been standing up for a while, but he had *never* taken any steps. Candy wondered if he going to be walking by the time his first birthday rolled around in a couple of months and there he was. She couldn't wait to show Goo. Candy grabbed RJ, along with his backpack and headed out. They made it home about thirty minutes later, and Candy was happy that there were leftovers in the fridge because she didn't feel like cooking shit. She managed to bring everything inside without having to make an extra trip to the car. Candy expected Ebony to be there, but she noticed the keys weren't on the counter and knew that she was still gone. She hoped that she was getting a better outlook on school.

Candy sat RJ in his playpen and then turned the TV on and changed the channel to the *Cartoon Network* while she went and changed clothes. She slipped out of her heels and suit and threw on a pair of Nike joggers and a tee shirt. When she walked back into the living room, the door opened and in walked Goo. He went straight to RJ and picked him up. Candy took him from Goo, and just as he was about to fuss, he noticed his son walking.

"Aww shit… lil homie walking now?" Goo beamed.

"Yep… they showed me at daycare as soon as I picked him up," Candy smiled.

"That's what's up. We might as well start on lil Raquisha now."

"Ra who? Boy please… you and the ghetto ass names you come up wit'. I ain't even having no more kids shit."

"I want a house full of kids," Goo said as he played with his son.

"Why? You hardly ever here," Candy fussed.

"Here you go wit' this shit… I told you I be in them streets for us."

"Whatever… wit' yo rude ass. I was calling to tell you *thank you* for the flowers earlier and you just blew me off."

"What flowers?" Goo quizzed.

"Those flowers," Candy pointed to the island where she had placed the beautiful arrangements.

Goo got up and went and looked at the flowers and then grabbed the card that was in them. Candy didn't even notice the card. The expression on Goo's face was one that he made when he was ready to spazz out.

"Who sent you these flowers?" he fumed.

"Nigga what you mean who sent them? You sent them," Candy said as she walked towards him.

She grabbed the card out of his hands and instantly saw why he was pissed off. Candy wished that she could disappear. How did she not see the card earlier? And who in the fuck hoped that she was single, still wanted her, and was still in love with her?

Chapter 11

Mark rode around, showing Kash the ropes. He loved the shit out of his city, but he really wished there wasn't so much violence. Most would say that he was a hypocrite for pushing drugs and even thinking like that, but what they didn't know was that most killings in Chicago were over the dumbest shit ever. You could accidentally step on someone's shoe and get killed over it. Looking at a nigga for too long was a threat to them and they would kill you for that. The worst thing was the drive-by shootings. A person could be going to KFC to get some got damn chicken and never make it back home. It was sad and Mark hoped that it would get better. He had one more spot that he wanted to take Kash too, but hunger had crept up on him, so he whipped into *Raisin Cane's* drive-thru.

"What you want?" he asked Kash before he rolled his window down.

"Ummm... I'll take a number one with a Sprite."

When the lady asked to take his order, Mark ordered two number ones, one with a Sprite and one with a Coke and then drove around. Kash attempted to hand him some money, but the look he gave her made her laugh and then apologize.

"Why you keep fuckin' wit' me?" he asked after he pulled up to the window.

"You know how I am," she replied.

"And *YOU KNOW* how I am. The fuck?" he paid for the food and then waited for their orders.

The worker handed Mark their drinks, and he placed them in the cup holders. When she passed the bag with the food, she smiled and rubbed Mark's hand. He smiled back, made eye contact with her, and passed Kash the bag without looking. She had been slick flirting since he pulled up, but touching his hand let him know that she was feeling him. Mark couldn't lie, she was a bad lil bitch.

"Don't make me fuck you up, bitch!" Kash fumed at the worker and broke Mark from the stare down him and the girl had going on.

"Oh... he yours? You look more like his mama than his woman," the girl took a shot.

"I'll show you mama... thot ass bitch," Kash unbuckled her seatbelt, but Mark grabbed her.

"Chill out," he told her and pulled off before she could say anything else to the girl.

He slick hated that he didn't get the chance to get the girl's number. She wasn't anybody that he would settle down with, but he damn sure would fuck her.

"Why you blocking and shit?" he laughed once he was back on the road.

"Nigga ain't nobody blocking. That shit was disrespectful. She don't know if we a couple or not," she rolled her eyes at him and handed him his fries followed by his chicken tenders.

"Seem like blocking to me... remember, you don't want my ass," he smirked.

"Whatever nigga... flirt when I ain't around," she said and then dived into her food.

"Women... I swear all y'all asses crazy," he mumbled and followed her lead by eating his food.

Mark made his way towards the last trap that he planned on showing Kash for the day. It took him almost thirty minutes to get there since it was on Douglas and Central Park, but that was cool because it gave both of them time to finish their food. When Mark pulled up to the spot, something seemed off. It seemed like some type of eerie feeling just washed over him. He made sure his piece was intact and then got out with Kash right by his side. Mark could tell from his peripheral that her hand was already on her gun. He made it to the door and was met by Timmy, one of the workers.

"What the fuck goin' on?" Mark asked when he saw the look on his face.

Timmy stepped to the side, and he saw two dead bodies lying on the floor. He listened as Timmy gave a rundown of how things were when he arrived. He told him that he had already called Malik and Goo and that they were on the way. Mark made his way through the spot and saw two more bodies. That was a total of four of their men that had been taken out. He was shocked and pissed as hell. They knew problems came in the street, but when he made it to the kitchen and saw the message that was written in blood, he knew that it was personal. If a nigga took time to write out, *You killed mine, and I'm killing all of yours,* that meant that shit had already gotten real right before their eyes.

"What in the fuck?" Mark heard his brother in-law fume from the living room.

He made his way back that way and saw Goo when he pulled up. Goo wasted no time hopping out of his car and coming inside. They surveyed the whole house the same as Mark had just done, and they all met back up in the living room. Kash was silent, but she observed everything just like everybody else.

"Y'all got surveillance over here right?" Kash finally broke her silence.

"Yeah but if a muthafucka really ran up in here and took out four of our men, they don't give a fuck about being caught. This shit is *personal*. Thing is, we've done so much shit, it ain't no got damn telling who it is," Malik analyzed.

"Yeah, that's true," Mark agreed.

"Well whoever the fuck it is better hope they get me before I get them and they whole muthafuckin family! *And that's on my mama!!*" Goo roared.

Chapter 12

Ebony sat in the back of her business management class and scrolled through Facebook. It was the third day of class and they were still going over the syllabus which was boring as fuck. She needed the professor to tell her exactly what was expected of her, so she could do it and go on with her life. It was Wednesday and thanks to Candy, she had two classes that day. Her big cousin insisted that she took one more class, just so she'd be set if anything ever happened; that way, she would still graduate on time. Ebony was cool with doing just the minimum. She did it to get through high school, where she graduated at the top of her class. Ebony figured that college couldn't be much different. After liking a few pictures and updating her status three times, Ebony's professor wrapped up the fake lecture and dismissed them. She gathered her Mac laptop and bag and headed towards the exit.

"Ms. Bell, I'm sorry that my class is boring you," Mr. Smith said as she slid past his desk.

"Oh, no, it's not. What makes you say that?" she asked.

"Well, the fact that your head stayed buried in your phone gave it away," he smiled.

"I am so sorry. It won't happen again," she apologized, turning red from embarrassment.

"I hope not. Now get out of here before I have you doing some extra credit," he smiled, winking his eye.

Ebony wasn't one hundred percent certain, but Mr. Smith had her feeling like he was flirting with her. It wasn't until she was talking to him up close that she realized how young he looked. He had a few gray streaks in his beard, but other than that, he looked youthful. She couldn't front, he was a very attractive man, and when she glanced down at the bulge in his jeans, he looked to be a *very blessed* man as well.

"I definitely wouldn't want that. I'll see you next week Professor," she replied, swinging her book bag over her right shoulder and heading towards the door.

Once she was out in the hall, she looked down at her phone and noticed that she had about fifteen minutes until her next class. She was unsure on how she would kill the extra time until her stomach began to growl. Ebony walked over to the vending machine and waited behind two classmates who were occupying it.

"Girl don't waste yo time. This dumb ass machine ain't gon' do nothing but take your money," one of the girls turned around and said to her.

"Damn! And I'm hungry," Ebony sighed.

"We are too. We got a few minutes until our next class, wanna go across the street to *Burger King* with us?" the other girl asked.

"Ummmm sure! Let's go," Ebony agreed and the three of them headed to eat.

"I'm Melissa and this my home girl Kelsey. We got business with you," Melissa stated.

"Hey y'all, I'm Ebony."

"You must not be from here?" Kelsey assumed.

"I'm not. How you know?" Ebony laughed as she zipped up her coat to help fight the Chicago wind.

"You talk all proper and shit," Melissa replied.

Ebony crossed the street laughing. She thought everyone from Chicago talked ghetto, which must explain why they consider her proper.

"I'm from Michigan girl. Right around the corner," Ebony finally replied as they entered *Burger King*.

There was no line, which made Ebony happy. Although she hated school, she still didn't want to be late, especially on the first week.

"Can I get a ummmmmm…. Number one with extra pickles and no onions or tomatoes please," Ebony ordered first.

After she placed her drink order, her classmates went and made their request. They waited for the food maybe five minutes before they headed back across the street to school.

"What class you got next?" Kelsey turned to Ebony and asked while they waited for the street light to turn.

"Girl accounting," she replied, rolling her eyes.

"Mr. Gray?" Melissa asked.

"Yup."

"Oh shit, we got him too. I guess we will be suffering together,"

The trio shared a laugh while they crossed the busy street. The three of them jumped back abruptly just as a black Maserati flew passed them.

"STUPID MOTHERFUCKER!" Ebony yelled at the car.

"Girl you better stop yelling like that. That type of shit will get you shot," Melissa informed her.

"Yelling will get me shot?" a confused Ebony asked.

"Not the yelling but the person you are yelling at," Kelsey advised.

"You gotta remember, she's not from here, so she don't know any better. But for future reference, when you see *that* Maserati, be cool cause those niggas don't play," Melissa stated firmly.

"What niggas?" Ebony asked.

"That was either Malik or Goo. Them the only niggas riding around like that in this city," she explained.

"Aw girl, Goo ain't nobody," Ebony laughed, waving them off.

"*NOBODY?* You crazy child. *That's* the man around here. As a matter of fact, he used to be Melissa's boo until he got her pregnant and played her to the left," Kelsey said, looking over at Melissa who had a mean mug on her face.

Ebony couldn't believe what she was hearing. There was no way that Candy's man was out there bogus like that. But according to the look of her new friend's face, everything that Kelsey said was the truth.

"Damn, that's crazy, but I know Goo. Well, I actually live with him," Ebony stated.

"*LIVE WITH HIM?*" Both Melissa and Kelsey said in unison.

"Yeah, that's my cousin's man."

"Wow! What a small world? How about we skip this class and get to know each other a little better FRIEND?" Melissa said, winking at Kelsey on the low as she placed her arm around Ebony's shoulder.

Chapter 13

Goo sat in the empty store that they used as a storage room and thought about all the shit that was going on. Just when he thought the bullshit was over, it seemed like it had just begun. The balls of the person who killed his workers had to be huge. Whoever ran into their spot, clearly didn't fear them or death. Goo looked up from his phone and grabbed his pistol that was on his waist when he heard the front door opening. Seconds later, he released his grip when he noticed Malik, Mark, and Kash walking in.

"It gotta be something serious, this nigga on time for a meeting," Mark said as he pulled up a seat.

"Nigga fuck you," Goo spat, eyeing Kash who wore a pair of leggings that showed every curve she had to offer.

Kash must have noticed Goo's eyes upon her because she gave him a slight grin before taking a seat.

"Aight look, y'all heard anything about those fuck niggas?" Malik questioned, taking a seat on the edge of the old wooden desk.

"Nope, all my niggas got eyes and ears to the streets but nothing came up yet," Mark answered.

"The person wrote that message in blood about y'all taking their people, does that give y'all any clue?" Kash inquired, looking around at the men in the room.

"Truthfully baby, we took so many lives, ain't no telling," Goo replied honestly while Malik and Mark shook their head in agreement.

"Yeah but we ain't got time to trip about some shit in the past. We need to figure out who's behind this before they hit us again," Malik finally spoke.

"But if the streets ain't talking, how the fuck we supposed to do that?" Mark quizzed.

"You know I don't give a fuck about these streets. These motherfuckers out here ain't loyal. The only motherfuckers I trust are the niggas in this room. I'll kill any motherfucker in order to get the answers I want," Goo snapped.

Goo scanned everyone's facial expression and stopped on Kash. He couldn't front. He was fascinated with her looks. He wondered how someone so sexy could be involved in the drug game. There were plenty of chicks out there in the streets, but Kash looked like she belonged on a niggas arm and *not* in his business. Goo's dick began to grow at the thought of her. He tried to control it because he figured that her and Mark had something going on, and he would never do no shit like that to his homie.

"Aight look, Lil Rob just texted me about some niggas that's been riding around the block. He said that they are currently parked on Hamlin and 16th. Mark ride with me, Kash hop in the car with Goo. Let's see what's to this," Malik said, getting up from the desk and walking towards the door.

Goo caught the look that Mark shot Kash but neither of them said anything. Goo checked his pockets for his keys and followed behind everyone. He locked the doors while Kash waited on the sidewalk. When he was done, Goo walked over and opened the door for Kash, helping her in.

"A thug and a gentleman huh?" she smirked.

"Shut up and get in," Goo laughed, shutting the door once she was fully inside.

He cranked up the car and headed towards Holy City in silence. He couldn't help but glance over at Kash occasionally while she starred into her phone.

"How you liking my city?" he asked her.

"*YO city?* Mark said this was *his* city," she giggled.

"Mark better get his bean head ass outta here. That nigga been in New York the past couple of years. This *MY* city," he explained.

"Look, I'm just telling you what the man told me. Don't beat my ass," she replied, holding both hands in the air as if she was surrendering.

"Nah, I wouldn't put my hands on you unless you wanted me to," he looked from the road briefly at her, licking his lips.

"Slow down killer, ain't you married?"

"Nah, Malik the only motherfucker tied down," he replied.

"They say a man who finds his queen officially becomes a king."

"It sound like you got that shit out of a fortune cookie. A nigga like me is a king without a queen."

"You only saying that because you haven't came across her yet," Kash stated.

Goo shrugged his shoulders and focused back on the road. They were about ten minutes from where they needed to be, but they were hitting all the traffic.

"Aye Kash!" Goo called out to her, but she didn't answer.

"Kash!" he yelled out again, this time looking away from the road and at her.

Goo's eyes bucked as he watched Kash load two nine millimeters.

"You good?" he asked, his eyes shifting back and forth.

"That black Dodge Charger been following us since we left the store. Turn into this alley right here," Kash instructed.

Goo looked at her out the side of his eye but did as she instructed, and just like clockwork, that Dodge Charger turned into the alley.

"Hit the brakes," she ordered.

Goo was hesitant at first, but by the look on Kash's face, he knew that he should listen. As soon as he did, she jumped out of Goo's car with guns in both hands and started blazing. Kash let off so many shots so quickly that the niggas in the car didn't have time to react. Shocked and turned on at the same time, Goo jumped out and emptied his clip, just to be on the safe side. The two of them walked over to car, and just like they expected, the two men in the front seat was slumped over dead. Sirens could be heard in a distance, indicating that they needed to get out of the area as fast as possible.

"Aight Kash, let's bounce," Goo yelled as he ran back to the car.

"Hold on."

Goo turned around and watched Kash reach into the car for something before jogging over to where he was. Before she could close the door, Goo sped off, blending into traffic like nothing ever happened.

"That shit crazy. I didn't even peep it," he admitted.

"It's cool. That's what I'm here for," she smiled.

"FUCK!" He yelled, this time hitting the steering wheel.

"What?"

"I still have no clue who the fuck these niggaz is."

"Well, this should help."

Kash tossed Goo the bloody cell phone that she grabbed out of the car.

"Some *KINGS* do need a *QUEEN* in their presence to get shit done," was the last thing she said before they pulled up to their destination.

Chapter 14

When Candy walked into her office, she noticed another beautiful arrangement. Learning from her last mistake, she instantly searched for a card and retrieved it as soon as she laid eyes on it. She knew exactly who it was when she read the last card. The argument that she had with Goo had been one for the books. His ass left and didn't return home until sometime over in the morning. Candy didn't bother checking the time because all it was going to do was start another argument. She just simply rolled over. Candy shrugged those thoughts off and read the card. The words made her mind drift back to her high school love, Lorenzo Edwards, and the last day that she saw him.

The day that Candy graduated from high school was so bittersweet. She was happy because of the accomplishments of her and classmates, but she was sad because it would be the last day that she saw her love. Lorenzo was a beast on the basketball court and could have been making millions in the NBA, but he chose a different route. He decided to go and play overseas. The money would still be good, but what drove him to do it was the experience. He offered for Candy to go with him, but she had dreams of her own.

"Don't look so sad. This should be one of happiest days of our lives," Lorenzo lifted her chin up and told her.

"How can I be truly happy when you're leaving me?" Candy said barely above a whisper.

"Babe... let's do what we said and celebrate. You know I will always love you, but we agreed not to let anyone or anything get in the way of dreams we had way before we fell in love."

"I know... it's easier said than done tho," Candy said as a tear slid down her cheek.

Lorenzo kissed her tears away and led her to his room. His parents had thrown him a graduation party, but you would have thought that it was for them as drunk as they got. Both of them were passed out drunk, and he helped them both to their room about an hour ago. Lorenzo kissed Candy and picked her up. He gently laid her down on the bed and undressed her. Moans escaped Candy's lips as he made a trail of kisses down her body. The feeling that he gave her was always phenomenal. He made Candy learn things about her body that she never knew. When his tongue massaged her clit, Candy came instantly. There was never a time that they had sex that Lorenzo didn't make sure that Candy came at least three times.

"Ummm… oh shit," Candy moaned as he entered her wetness.

As they made love, she enjoyed every minute but couldn't help but to be sad. Candy felt like a piece of her was leaving. In reality, for the past three years, her and Lorenzo had been inseparable. Lorenzo was everything that a woman dreamt of. Candy slept in his arms that night, and the next day the tears wouldn't stop as she watched him leave. They promised to keep in touch, and they did. The last time that she talked to Lorenzo was a few years ago when he told her that he had gotten married. She knew that he was in a relationship, but Candy had no idea why he never told her that he was planning on getting married. She wished him the best and decided that it was time for the calls to stop so that he could focus on his new life. She met Goo shortly afterwards, and he filled the void that she never knew was so deep.

Candy's intercom buzzed and pulled her from her thoughts. It was her assistant telling her that the RJ's daycare was on the line. She had no idea what they could have wanted, but Candy picked up the phone right away after stuffing the card from the flowers into her purse.

"Hi… is everything okay?" Candy instantly inquired.

"Ms. Williams… there's been an accident, and we need you to meet us at the hospital. I'm so…"

Candy had grabbed her purse, phone, and keys and was out of the door before the sentence was complete. She knew that they had to have taken her baby to Rush because it was the closest to where they were. Candy turned her hazard lights on and sped the entire way. She called Goo twice, but he didn't answer his phone. As a mother, Candy didn't even have time to get mad at his ass. She just prayed that there wasn't anything serious wrong with her baby. Fifteen minutes later, Candy arrived at the hospital, and God must have been on her side because there was a vacant parking space in the front.

She hopped out and made her way inside. Candy bumped into several people along the way and apologized without stopping. Getting to her baby was top priority because the feeling that she got during the drive to the hospital put her on edge. Before she could get to the desk, she spotted Mrs. Johnson, the director. Upon seeing her, Candy knew that something was terribly wrong.

"Ms. Williams…. I'm so sorry this happened."

Candy saw tears form in Mrs. Johnson's eyes, and before she even knew what was going on, tears were falling down her own cheeks.

"RJ crawled and grabbed a cup of bleach, and when Sharon turned around, he had drunk some before she got to him…"

"What the fuck??" Candy fumed.

A doctor appeared before Mrs. Johnson could reply to Candy.

"I'm Dr. Washington. You must be the mother of the infant," he extended his hand and then motioned for them to follow him.

All kinds of thoughts ran through Candy's mind. She knew accidents happened, but they better prayed that her son was okay or someone was going to have *hell* to pay, and it wouldn't be Goo taking care of anyone, it would be her. Candy listened as the doctor explained how they had flushed RJ's system and gave him antibiotics. Dr. Washington told her that swallowing bleach was common, but he did let her know that the amount that RJ had taken in was uncommon because of the taste, and he had drunk a good bit. She was informed that her son would have some nausea and vomiting, and they would keep him for a couple of days to make sure that he was okay. Candy was relieved to hear that her son would be okay, but she was still hurt and truth be told, a little angry. Just knowing that her son was okay allowed her to receive the hug that Mrs. Johnson gave her.

"I'm so sorry this happened. I can assure you that it will be handled," Mrs. Johnson told her.

Candy didn't reply. She honestly didn't know what to say. She just nodded her head.

"Can I see my son?" she asked the doctor.

"Sure… he's a little sedated, so he's probably sleeping, but you can be with him now," Dr. Washington informed her.

Candy followed him to RJ's room with Mrs. Johnson right by her side. When she walked in, tears streamed down her face nonstop. She thanked God that things didn't turn out worse than they did. Candy's emotions were all over the place. RJ was resting peacefully, but she couldn't help but to kiss all over him. Mrs. Johnson did the same thing once she was done. She was one of the sweetest women that Candy knew, which was why she chose her facility to care for her son.

"I'm gonna let you enjoy him, and we will talk soon. This is very unfortunate, but *please* think carefully before removing him. I understand as a mother myself that this is a hard decision, but just know that you will be reimbursed for all childcare fees that you have paid this year and the rest of the year is free."

Being a lawyer, Candy knew what Mrs. Johnson was doing, and she couldn't do anything but respect her for it. People sued over the smallest things, but it really never crossed her mind. The only thing she wanted was for her son to be okay, and until he was up running around again, he wouldn't be normal to her.

"I understand, Mrs. Johnson. We'll be in touch."

Candy pulled her phone from her purse and called her mom when Mrs. Johnson left. Her mom was the level headed one and told Candy that accidents happened and told her that she would be there soon to check on them. Mrs. Williams had helped her daughter more than she knew. Candy pulled the chair that was in the room right beside the bed and sat down. Goo hadn't called back, so she decided to call him again. After getting the same results, Candy shook her head and the anger that she had pushed to the side resurfaced. Being angry wasn't going to help anything, so Candy pulled the card from her purse and dialed the number that was on it. If Goo couldn't or wouldn't answer the phone, she knew someone who would.

Chapter 15

Shit had been getting real in the streets and Mark didn't want to admit it out loud, but he had a strong feeling that some deeper shit was about to go down. He couldn't put his finger on it, but he tried to figure the shit out just like the rest of the team. Since he finally had a little moment to chill, he shot Malik a text and told him to meet him at *The Bar Below* in Chicago. He wanted to meet up with his brother in-law for a couple of reasons and that was why he didn't invite Goo. Mark parked, put his coat on, got out, and then headed inside. The bar was packed, so he sat in the first booth that was available. It was only Wednesday, but it appeared that he wasn't the only one in need of a few drinks.

The waitress walked over and Mark went ahead and ordered two double shots of Remy on the rocks. As soon as she walked away, Malik sat down across from him.

"What's up bro?" he spoke.

"Man shit… I'm glad my sister let you out."

"Nigga don't get it twisted. You know I got Micah lil ass in check."

"Yeah right," Mark replied, and they both laughed.

The waitress was back in no time with their drinks, and Mark went ahead and ordered another round, along with some hot wings before she left. Mark verbalized a few of his feelings about the street shit to Malik, and he found out that his brother felt the exact same way. Both of them agreed that it was time to step their game up and find the head of the source before any more of their men were taken out. They had taken enough losses and weren't up to taking any more. Mark got silent after they talked about business and tried to figure out the best approach to his next issue, but he didn't have to think long because Malik beat him to it.

"Damn… what else on your mind… wait, let me guess, it's Kash ain't it. I see the way you be looking at her and shit."

"Kash is like my lil sister, but I'll always look out for her."

"Nigga that's the shit every nigga say when it's a girl they wanna fuck but can't. Same as these hoes with that *he's just like my brother* shit," Malik waved him off.

"You sayin' I can't fuck her? Watch then…"

"I just proved my point. If you didn't already wanna do the shit, you wouldn't have agreed that fuckin' fast," Malik drank the rest of his drink.

"Fuck you nigga," Mark did the same with his drink just as the waitress brought round two along with the wings.

"But on the real though, she *is* like my sister. You think Goo would fuck wit' her?" Mark continued.

"Oh shit… *this* the real issue and it *ain't* shit I'm tryna be in the middle of."

"That's yo boy though… and it ain't on no hating type shit, but him fuckin' with Kash just wouldn't be good for business," Mark explained.

"I can't argue wit' that, but Goo is a different kinda nigga. He would never let a bitch come between business."

"Kash *ain't no bitch*, bro."

"I didn't mean it like that… damn she got you gone. Listen, until y'all stop playing games, you *need* to get you some pussy. Look at them hoes up there at the bar. They keep looking this way on the slick side. Ima head out and I guarantee you, one of 'em coming this way. Go get you some pussy… on me," Malik said as he stood up and placed two hundred dollar bills on the table in front of Mark and laughed.

"Fuck you nigga," Mark told him, but Malik only continued to laugh and went ahead and left.

If Mark didn't know any better, he would have sworn Malik went and told one of the bitches to come to the booth because it wasn't two minutes after he left that one of them had his taken spot. He knew better than that though and chunked it up to his brother in-law knowing women. Even thought he was committed to his sister, Mark wasn't a fool. He knew Malik stayed in the loop on every damn thing.

"What's your name, handsome?" she smiled at him.

"Names aren't important at the moment. What's important is that you 'bout to meet me at the *Holiday Inn* and let me fuck the shit outta you," Mark replied.

An hour later, Mark walked into room 359 with the unknown female right behind him. He didn't know how often she hooked up with and fucked niggas from the bar, but that wasn't his concern. All Mark had on his mind was busting a *much needed* nut. As much as Mark hated to admit that Malik was right, he knew that he was, which was why he took him up on his offer. No words were exchanged once the doors were closed. Mark dropped his pants and boxers and the girl wasted no time taking him into her mouth. He didn't have a clue what her name was, but for the time being, it was *Super Head* because she was giving him the business. Mark fell back onto the bed because his knees gave out.

The way that she stopped and looked up at him, let him know that she knew her head game was A-1. Shorty had skills out of this world, and it was safe to say that she was giving him the best head that he had ever received; and, he thought that he had been living life. His dick began to pulsate in her mouth, and Mark knew that he was about to come. A few seconds later, she swallowed all of his kids and then sucked him hard again. Mark reached into his pants pockets and grabbed a condom after he was completely hard again. The female laid down on the bed, and Mark entered her with ease. She wasn't tight as he liked, but the memory of the head was all he needed to keep going. Mark kept his promise and fucked the shit out of her. They went through three pack of condoms, and when they were done, she sucked his head to perfection once again. Mark had every intention of it being a one night stand, but that head had him gone, so he asked her for her name and number. Once he stored her name and number, Mark washed up and dipped out with a smile on his face. He knew what the business was, so he didn't leave without dropping shorty off with a few bills. He damn sure knew that he would be calling her again. Sooner rather than later.

Chapter 16

Ever since Ebony joined forces with Melissa and Kelsey, life in Chicago wasn't so bad after all. The first day they met, they skipped class and hung out at Melissa's condo, where they listened to music, smoked weed, and had a few shots of Patron. At first, Ebony felt bad for missing out on class, but she made a promise to herself that she would study hard next week and make up for it. Now there it was, almost a week later but instead of studying like she vowed, she was getting dressed on a school night to hit the club.

"Aw shit, you fine. Where the fuck you going?" Candy asked as she walked passed the bedroom.

"Me and some classmates are going to study and then possibly out for drinks." she semi-lied.

"That's how y'all dress to study?" Candy questioned, eyeing her baby cousin suspiciously.

Ebony let out a long sigh and rolled her eyes. "I *JUST* said that we are going out for drinks."

"Girllll, you better watch yo ......"

Candy words were cut short when her phone chimed. Ebony noticed the way her eyes lit up as she read what she assumed was a text message.

"Damn girl, you ok?" she asked.

"Oh, my bad, what was I saying.... Aw yeah.... Have fun!" Candy beamed as she walked away with her face buried into her phone.

"Goo must be doing something right," Ebony whispered but apparently not low enough.

"FUCK GOO!" is what Candy yelled out from down the hall, causing Ebony to laugh.

After slipping on a pair of black peep-toe red bottoms, Ebony walked over to the full-length mirror and did a full spin. Dressed in an all-black fitted body-con dress from *Fashion Nova*, her hair flat ironed bone straight, and her makeup beat. She knew that she was fine and if you said she wasn't, you were a *got-damn* lie. Ebony began to dance in the mirror, twerking the little ass that she did have before stopping abruptly. She thought she heard her phone vibrating, her thoughts were confirmed when she glanced over at it lightening up on the bed. She quickly made her way over to answer it before it stopped ringing.

"We outside!" Melissa advised her before ending the call.

Ebony grabbed her clutch and headed out the door, but not before placing a soft kiss on RJ's forehead, who was asleep on the couch. It was his first day home from the hospital. When Candy told Ebony what happened, it broke her heart. RJ was the sweetest little boy in the world, and she was happy to know that he was alright. Ebony walked slowly down the stairs to Melissa's Ford Focus. It had snowed that morning and rained that afternoon, so the ground was slippery. After making it to the car successfully, she hopped in the back seat, where the three of them, including Kelsey, headed to get their night started.

"So, what club are we blessing our presence with tonight?" Ebony asked as she took the blunt from Melissa.

"Club Escape," she replied, looking over at Kelsey smiling.

"Never heard of it. I hope it be lit," Ebony replied before taking a hard pull from the blunt.

"Trust us, it is." The both of them replied in unison before Melissa turned up the radio.

"Said, "Lil bitch, you can't fuck with me if you wanted to"
These expensive, these is red bottoms, these is bloody shoes
Hit the store, I can get 'em both, I don't wanna choose
And I'm quick, cut a nigga off, so don't get comfortable, look
I don't dance now, I make money moves
Say I don't gotta dance, I make money move
If I see you and I don't speak, that means I don't fuck with you
I'm a boss, you a worker, bitch, I make bloody moves."

Cardi B's voice blasted through the speakers, getting the ladies in club mode. It felt like it had been forever since the last time she'd been out. She was long overdue for some ratchet fun, and by looking at the men that was entering the club as they searched for a park, Ebony could tell she was going to no doubt enjoy herself.

"I can't wait to get these thirsty ass niggas to buy me a drink," Kelsey stated as she opened up the front door once they parked.

"You sure they the ones thirsty?" Melissa asked, causing Ebony to laugh however, Kelsey didn't find anything funny.

"Aw be cool, you know she's joking," Ebony replied, locking arms with Kelsey as they walked out of the parking lot, across the street to the club.

The line wasn't as long as she expected, which made her happy. They stood around and waited until it was their turn, which was about five minutes later. Ebony watched as everyone made their way in, especially keeping her eyes on the guys. It seemed as if every nigga that walked passed her was made of money. The designer clothes and the icy jewelry that clung to their body, made her pussy wet. Chicago wasn't her favorite place in the world but those Michigan's niggas didn't have shit on the men here. Once they made their way in, they quickly snatched up a table not too far from the bar. The dance floor was packed and the club was beautiful. Ebony could tell that the owner took pride in their establishment because that place was a palace compared to the hole in the wall clubs she was used to.

"Y'all want something to drink?" Melissa yelled over the music.

"I'm good but I'll go with you," Ebony replied, handing her clutch to Kelsey who stayed behind to keep their table.

There were a few people in line ahead of them, but the bartender was like superwoman, the way she made those drinks and dished them out so quickly.

"What can I get ya?" she asked with a smile.

"Can I have a double shot of Patron?" Melissa ordered.

"And what about you pretty lady?" she asked Ebony.

"Oh! I'm good. I'm not much of a drinker," she informed her.

Without saying any further words, the bartender fixed Melissa's drink, and before Ebony could blink, they were headed back to their table. They vibed along with the music until Uncle Luke's hit song in the 90's *Do Do Brown* came on. Like clockwork, the trio ran onto the dance floor and began a twerk fest. The entire club erupted, men picked their favorite dancer to grope on while each woman tried to out dance each other. Ebony was so caught up, she didn't even bother to turn around to see whose hard dick was pressed up on her ass. When the song was over, Ebony worked up a sweat and was now thirsty. She looked around and spotted both Melissa and Kelsey flirting with some guys. Not wanting to cock-block, she headed over to the bar to get a bottle of water. As soon as she walked up, a female was getting up, making a stool available. Tired from dancing and those Christian Louboutin's hurting her feet, she quickly snatched up the seat.

"Ya back huh?" the bartender asked, sliding a napkin in front of her.

"Yup, let me get a bottle of water."

The bartender winked her eyes and headed to the small refrigerator where she grabbed the cold Dasani bottle. Ebony slid her a ten-dollar bill and told her to keep the change before gulping down the drink.

"Damn baby," she heard a male's voice say from behind her.

Ebony rolled her eyes before placing the water bottle on the bar and turning around. There was a dude standing behind her with long dreads and tattoos all over his face. He looked to be straight out of a gangster music video. She looked him up and down before standing to her feet. Ebony attempted to walk away but was stopped by the guy standing behind her.

"Don't be rude lil bitch," he snapped, pulling her by the arm over to him.

"Nigga don't touch me," she snapped back.

"Bitch, I'll beat yo ass," he yelled, drawing attention to them.

"You gon' do what?"

Ebony looked behind the rude hoodlum and stared into the eyes of her dream man. She had only crossed paths with him once before, but his face is something that she'd never forget. The hoodlum turned around ready to go off but something humbled him really quick, whereas he became speechless.

"Nigga don't make me repeat myself!" Malik spoke again.

"I- I- I'm sorry Malik, I didn't know..." the hoodlum stuttered.

"You didn't know what? Ain't shit to know. You sitting here disrespecting a female like the shit cool."

The hoodlum hung his head low like he was being disciplined by big momma.

"Now apologize," Malik ordered.

"I apologize for the rude shit I said a few seconds ago."

That hood shit went out the window. That nigga went from *The Game* to *Ru Paul* in a matter of seconds. Malik whispered something in the man's ear and seconds later, he was gone.

"Thank you," Ebony blushed.

"Nah you good. You Candy cousin right?" he inquired.

"Yeah, you remember huh?" she asked.

"I don't forget faces," he stated, looking down at the Rolex on his arm.

Just as Ebony was about to say something else, the bartender yelled out to Malik.

"Aye bossman, can I get you anything?" she asked.

"I'm good Krystal but thank you," he replied back.

"Bossman huh?" Ebony hissed.

"Yeah, this my shit, and I hope you enjoying your night. Let me know if you need anything," he smiled before walking off.

Ebony was left standing there stuck. She felt her panties soaking up the moisture that was between her legs. She turned around to find her friends but laid eyes on the bathroom instead. She rushed over before it got too crowed. Once a stall was available, she went inside, pulled down her panties, and began to massage her clit. It was something about Malik that drove her crazy. She had never wanted a man so bad in her life, and at that point, she was willing to do whatever it took to get him, even if that meant ending his marriage.

Chapter 17

Goo pulled his dick out and laid on his back, out of breath. Him and Candy had just finished round two, and Goo was pretty sure that the last nut was going to bless him with a baby girl. He knew that now was not the time to be thinking about expanding their family, especially since shit had been rocky with them as of lately. Goo loved Candy and RJ was his life, but with all the shit going on in the streets, he had been neglecting them and he knew it. Rico felt like shit when he got the message about RJ being in the hospital. The thought of life without his *mini-me* was something he couldn't fathom. After his son's accident, he said *fuck everything in those streets*; he was finally going to make shit right at home. It was day three and Goo had only left their crib to get shit for Candy and RJ. He gave all his hood problems to Malik, Mark, and Kash for the time being. He knew he had to make shit right and that's what he planned on doing.

"Come here, why you all the way over there?" Goo asked, pulling Candy towards him.

Although Candy didn't put up a fight, Goo still had a feeling that she didn't want to be near.

"You know I love you Candace," he whispered in her ear.

"I love you too Rico," she mumbled back.

"But I gotta get up and get dressed," she continued, pulling the covers off of her.

"Oh yeah, where you going?" he questioned.

"I- ummmm- I –I gotta take care of some business," she stuttered.

Goo wasn't sure how Candy was so successful at being a lawyer because he knew every time she was lying. Goo released the grip he had around his girlfriend and watch her move about the room.

"You going to see the nigga who sent you the flowers?" he blurted out.

The look on Candy's face was priceless. Ever since those flowers were sent, Goo never spoke another word about it. It's not that he had forgotten or he didn't care, it simply slipped his mind. He was waiting on the right time to bring it up again and there it was. Since Goo had been home, Candy had been moving differently. Her face stayed buried in her phone. She was smiling at shit for no reason. Goo reflected back to when he was a shorty before his OG was killed by her bitch ass boyfriend. When she first started fucking with him, she was acting the same way. Maybe it was his cockiness that didn't have him worried initially, but now, he needed to address the shit.

"You heard what the fuck I said Candy. What's up with the nigga who sent you the flowers?" he asked again, this time getting out of the bed.

"It's nothing Goo," she replied, blowing him off.

"Mannnnnnnn......"

Goo tried to calm himself down before he went off. The fact that she was lying to him in his face is what pissed him the fuck off.

"Look, who sent you the flowers?" he asked again, this time in a much calmer manner.

Candy let out a long sigh before turning around facing him.

"This guy I dated when I was younger. He's married and lives overseas," she explained.

"So why the fuck *his* married ass sending *my* bitch flowers?" he snapped.

"Same reason *yo* married ass was fucking with me," she snapped back.

Goo could tell by the look on Candy's face that she regretted her response immediately, but it was too late, she had already said too much.

"So you gon' fuck that married nigga like you fucked me?"

Candy paused in her tracks and slowly turned around to face him again.

"Rico, you need to get the fuck out my face before this shit escalates but to answer your question, NO. I'm not fucking him because unlike you, he was man enough to tell me that he was married *before* he pursued me."

Those words felt like daggers to Goo's heart. He could look into Candy's eyes and still see the hurt in them. Although it had been almost three years, she still hadn't gotten over it.

"Look baby, I'm sorry, but I can't help but wonder who sending my girl flowers. I know that I've fucked up in the past and probably still fucking up now, but I'm trying to make it better. I'm trying to make it work. I had plans for us tonight and the fact that you just dipping out on me is pissing me off," he explained, pulling her close to him.

The two of them stood in the middle of the bedroom still naked, just staring into each other eyes before Candy spoke up.

"I'm sorry, I wasn't aware that you had plans, and besides, we have no sitter for RJ. Monica has plans tonight," Candy said, referring to their regular sitter.

"I'm ten steps ahead of you. I paid Ebony to watch him for us already tonight, so what's the next excuse?"

"There's no excuse. I'll cancel my plans," she smiled, finally warming up.

"Aight bet. Grab that red dress that I hid in Ebony's closet, along with those Giuseppe heels that's under her bed. Be ready in an hour," Goo ordered, kissing her on the forehead before heading to the bathroom.

After waiting an hour plus an extra thirty minutes, Candy was finally dressed and ready to go. Goo looked at his lady and couldn't help but smile, she looked beautiful. He grabbed her by the hand and headed to her favorite restaurant *Morton's Steakhouse*, downtown on Wacker. Goo held her hand during the entire ride; however, something in Candy's phone continued to snatch her attention. He decided to let it go for the time being but definitely planned on saying something if it continued.

They arrived at the restaurant thirty minutes later and were immediately seated, although the place was packed. One of Goo's friend's old lady was the manager there, and she came through with the reservations. They were placed in a nice cozy corner away from the mayhem that usually took place inside the five-star restaurant.

"Oh, you a gentleman tonight huh?" Candy smiled as he pulled out her chair.

"I'm trying shorty," Goo laughed before taking his own seat.

Less than a minute later, a young male waiter appeared with their menus, requesting their drink orders. Both Goo and Candy settled for water along with baked escargot and prosciutto wrapped mozzarella for their appetizer. They continued to look over the menus until they made up their minds regarding their main course.

"So how have work been baby?" Goo asked, placing his phone down before staring across the table at Candy.

"These cases kicking my ass. I was thinking about taking a trip but with the shit going on with RJ, I'll feel horrible leaving him right now," she explained.

"RJ good. He's a strong baby, but I do think you should get away. I mean, even if it's not to another country, just do some chill shit with yo girls."

"You know what? You right. Ima hit up Micah tomorrow. Maybe like a girl's night, something real cute," Candy grinned.

The couple discussed a few more things before the waiter returned with their appetizers.

"I'm going to wash my hands, I'll be back," she stated before looking at something in her phone.

She placed the iPhone 7 plus face down on the table and left. Goo looked around to make sure she was gone before flagging down the waiter.

"Aye, can you tell the manager Tiffany, Goo said come here," he asked once the waiter appeared.

Just as he was about to leave to hunt her down, she came walking up to the table smiling.

"You ready?" she asked.

"As ready as I'm going to get," Goo replied, reaching inside his pocket and handing Tiffany a black velvet box.

Tiffany eyes lit up when she opened the box that contained the five carats, diamond cut engagement ring.

"Oh my Goooodddddd!" she squealed.

"I'll make sure my crew do their part and congratulations," she continued before walking off.

Goo palms began to sweat as he prepared for the main event. There was no doubt in his mind that he wanted to spend the rest of his life with Candy, it was now time to prove it. Goo's phone vibrated on the table. He was pretty sure that it was Micah calling to make sure he didn't fuck this up. He had reached out to her two days ago about proposing to Candy, and she went crazy. Micah picked out the ring and even planned the proposal. Goo felt the whole engagement ring in the food shit was corny, but it was last minute so he flowed with it. The phone vibrated again but this time, he realized that it wasn't his phone, it was Candy's. Without giving it much thought, he picked up the phone and read the message that was on the screen.

Lorenzo: I love you Candy. Always have and always will...

Goo felt the veins in his head about to pop out. His chest felt like it was filled with fire as he reread the message again. There was a sharp pain in his chest that he had never experienced before, but he decided to play it cool because now was not the time or place. He quickly sat her phone back down and took a sip from his glass just as she walked up.

"That damn bathroom was crowed. Did he come back to take our order yet?" she asked before sitting down.

"Nah but I'll be back," he replied, getting up from his seat.

He had to catch Tiffany before it was too late. There was no way he was about to wife that bitch after reading that text message. To say he wasn't hurt would be a lie. As a matter of fact, this was his first heartbreak and it damn sure was going to be his last. The old Goo was back, and it wasn't shit nobody could do about that.

Chapter 18

Candy watched as Goo rushed away, and she knew her man well enough to know that he was pissed the fuck off. The reason why was a mystery to her though. A few minutes later, Goo returned to the table, sat down, and grabbed his phone.

"What's wrong with you?" Candy finally asked after he ignored her for about two or three minutes while being on his phone.

"Shit," he replied without looking up.

"So you expect me to believe that?"

"It really don't even matter. I just wanna eat and get the fuck outta here," he shrugged.

Candy just stared at him. She thought about how she had just sent Lorenzo a text a little while ago telling him that she felt like it would be best if they didn't start anything that they both knew wasn't right. He hadn't texted her back, but she knew that he would understand because he was just that type of person. Candy took a sip of her water and then picked up her phone since Goo was ignoring her. She clicked on the message icon and noticed that Lorenzo had replied to her text, but it had been read. Candy instantly knew that Goo had read the text. She never had a lock code on her phone because she didn't need one. But in that moment, Candy wished that she would have had one.

"So you went through my phone, Rico?"

"Hell naw I ain' go through your phone. I did look at the text message the married man sent you though," he stared at her with fire in his eyes.

"Did you look at the message that I sent him?"

"What the fuck I just say?" Goo roared and pounded his fist on the table.

"Who the fuck you think you talking to?" Candy matched his anger.

"Is everything okay here?" a manager walked up to the table and asked.

Both Candy and Goo ignored her and continued to stare at each other. The tension and anger were at an all time high, and Candy knew that it would probably be best if they just went ahead and left. Their appetizers were placed in front of them, but Candy's appetite was long gone. The manager and the waiter finally walked away, and Candy decided to say what was on her mind.

"You be in the streets doing *any and every* fuckin' thing that you want to, but you wanna trip about ONE text message from a nigga. A text that said he will always love me. Did you stop to think that maybe, just maybe, I was telling him that I didn't think we should talk anymore because I didn't wanna jeopardize my relationship? Nah, you didn't because everything is always about Rico Grady."

After Candy expressed her feelings, Goo simply went back to looking at his phone and dismissed her like she was the scum of the Earth. Candy picked up her glass of water and threw it in Goo's face.

"Bit..."

"Call me a bitch and watch how I fuck yo whole life up," Candy threatened.

"Get the fuck out my face Candy," Goo spat.

"I'll do better than that. I'll get the fuck out of your life," Candy matched his venom and walked away.

Candy walked to the front of the restaurant. On the way, she clicked on the Lyft app and requested a ride. It said that it would take five minutes, so she paced back and forth while she waited. Instead of going home, Candy was going to Micah's house because the way that she was feeling, she didn't need to see or be anywhere near Goo. A few seconds later, Goo walked right by her and out of the restaurant without acknowledging her whatsoever. Candy was thankful that her gun wasn't on her because the way that she was feeling, it was a good chance that she would have shot his ass. Her phone rang letting her know that her ride was outside, so she exited the restaurant and got in. Candy texted Micah and let her know that she was on her way, and instead of texting back, Micah called.

"I'm so happy for you... I can't wait..."

"We'll talk when I get there because the shit that I wanna say, don't need to be heard by nobody else," Candy cut her off.

"Damn... what the fuck happened?"

"I'll be there soon," Candy replied and hung up.

She didn't mean to be rude to her girl, but she was dead ass serious about what she said. The lawyer side of her was in full thinking mode on ways to take Goo's ass out. An image of RJ popped into Candy's head, and it softened her heart momentarily. About twenty minutes later, the driver pulled up at Malik and Micah's place and Candy got out without saying anything. It wasn't like her to be rude, but she was having a bad day and anyone could get it at that point. She walked up to the door and Micah opened it before she could knock.

"What in the hell happened?"

"I wanna kill Rico Grady. He makes me fucking sick," Candy fumed.

"This was supposed to be a great night for y'all... what went wrong?" Micah quizzed.

"He read a text message on my phone and fucked up the whole night. If he was gon' go looking for shit, the least coulda did was read the whole damn convo."

"Wait, who you been texting?" Micah led her to the living room.

"Damn... what the fuck happened wit' y'all now?" Malik appeared and asked.

"Fuck your boy," Candy spat.

"Y'all gon' be alright. I'm goin' to meet that nigga now," Malik kissed Micah on the forehead and left out.

"So who you been texting?" she asked again once Malik was gone.

Candy sighed and then filled Micah in.

"Lorenzo was my high school sweetheart. He sent me flowers and we been conversing, but that's it. You know I been pissed because Goo lives in the streets, so it was like a breath of fresh air to me. For the past few days, Goo has been at the house and then he said he had something planned. I saw the effort that he was putting forth, so I told Lorenzo that I felt like we needed to stop talking because I was in a relationship. He texted while I was in the bathroom at restaurant and Goo read the text," Candy showed Micah the text.

"So… was this before or after the proposal?" Micah quizzed.

"What proposal?"

"I helped Goo set this whole night up. He took you to your favorite restaurant to propose to you, girl… I've been waiting to hear how everything went for hours now."

"Goo actually bought a ring?"

"Yeesss… he put in a lot of work to make this night special.

Hearing Micah say that made Candy feel a little bad, but it still didn't take away from the fact that their relationship had been on the rocks before Lorenzo even popped into the picture. Candy loved Goo with everything within her, but she knew that she wouldn't be able to deal with his ways forever.

"So what y'all gon' do?" Micah inquired.

"It's over Micah. I can't keep going in circles with Goo. He made it clear that I ain't shit anyway. The nigga walked out of the restaurant and left me. Not caring how I was getting home," Candy finally cried.

Micah pulled her into her arms and allowed her to cry it all out. Candy was very headstrong, but the truth was, she didn't want to lose Goo. She just wanted him to be at home more and realize the harm that he was causing himself as well as his family.

"Y'all are gonna be okay. Both of y'all just need some time a part. That will make both of y'all see that it ain't shit else out there," Micah consoled her.

"No friend… I saw the way he looked at me. He hates me and right now, I hate him. I'm just gonna focus on my son. I've been thinking about leaving Chicago anyway. I don't wanna raise my son here when he gets older, and we both know Goo will never leave, so it's probably best to end things now instead of dragging them out."

"Listen... we not about to worry about all that right now. Let's have a girl's night tomorrow and cheer you up. I'll even invite your little cousin."

"You don't even like Ebony," Candy laughed for the first time.

"This is true, but I love you and she's your cousin, and I'll do anything for you. Text me her number and we'll set everything up," Micah smiled.

"But on another note... what does Mr. Lorenzo look like since he done came in here and fucked shit up?" Micah smirked.

Candy smiled and pulled her phone out. She clicked the Facebook app and found his page and let Micah scroll through his profile.

"Damn... Lorenzo fine as hell. Goo might better watch out," Micah bubbled.

"Especially since he's going through a divorce," Candy finally admitted to her friend.

Chapter 19

For the past few days, Mark had been getting head from his new little fuck buddy. Kash had been on his ass and saying that he was slipping; but he knew that she was just jealous because he hadn't been giving her the time that she was used to. To be honest, he was still a little on edge about the way that he had seen her and Goo looking at and acting around each other, but he knew that he had to shrug it off and keep the business running smoothly. When Kash called him earlier that morning, Mark told her that he was going to take her to lunch. No matter what, the relationship that he had with Kash was one that he never wanted to end, so Mark knew that he had to get his shit together. Mark pulled into the parking lot of the funeral home and parked. He got out and headed inside and was greeted by his sister.

"Hey big head," Mesha spoke and then hugged him.

"Hey sis… you been MIA."

"I know you ain't talking. I didn't expect you to move out so fast… guess you just had to be near Kash huh," Mesha teased.

"What? We was talking about you and yo ass gon' flip it on me."

"I'm just sayin'… I like her though. She seems like a great catch, and mom would love her too I'm sure," Mesha smiled.

Just the mention of his mom made Mark both happy and sad at the same time. He sure did miss her. Mark made a mental note to go and grab some flowers and take out to her grave. The best thing about their funeral home, they had a florist on sight, so after Mark finished chopping it up with his sister, he went to the florist and requested a spray for his mom's grave as well as a dozen yellow roses in a vase. He made his way to his dad's office and found him on the computer. His dad closed the computer real fast, and it made Mark wonder what the hell he was doing. His dad, just the like the rest of the family, had been through a lot with the passing of their mom and how quickly everything happened. Mark knew that it was harder on their dad than he admitted and the gambling addiction he had was a lot to handle as well. Mark didn't want to think the worst of his dad, but he wondered if he was back gambling after he had paid off all of his debts for him.

"What up pops?" he quizzed.

"Just working son… and trying to put some stuff together," Michael replied.

"Aight… how's everything going wit' the books and shit here?" Mark asked in an attempt to see where his dad's head was really at.

"Everything is great. The girls pretty much take care of all that. You know how Micah is," Michael laughed.

Mark laughed as well because Micah didn't take shit lightly. He decided to shrug off his thoughts and prayed that his dad was telling the truth. Mark wasn't the type to go looking for shit and checking behind people; he knew that everything always came to the light no matter what so he let most shit be. After talking to his dad for about twenty more minutes and agreeing to go to a Chicago Bulls game soon, Mark went and grabbed the flowers from the florist and left. He shot Kash a text and let her know that he would be there in about fifteen minutes. He decided that he would scoop her up, go by the cemetery, and then head to the *Hibachi Grill*. Mark knew that if he asked her what she wanted to eat, she was going to say it didn't matter. That was one of things Mark would never understand about women. They asses was always hungry but never knew what the hell they wanted to eat.

He left their place of business and immediately noticed a car creeping up behind him. Mark felt for his piece and assured that it was still in place, which it was and began to slow down. Being the different nigga that he was, speeding up wasn't what he did. He damn near came to a complete stop, and a few minutes later, the car did a U-turn in the road.

"Pussy ass niggas," he mumbled and then pulled back off into traffic.

Twenty minutes later, Mark pulled up at Willow Lake Apartments and called Kash. She came out almost immediately and hopped into his car.

"Hey big head," she spoke and kissed him on the jaw.

"Someone's in a good mood I see," he smiled and spoke back.

Mark thought about what Mesha had said earlier, but he kept it to himself.

"What you want to eat?"

"Hmm... I don't know. It don't really matter though," she said.

"Women," Mark mumbled as he got back on the highway.

"Don't start," Kash rolled her eyes.

"I'm just sayin'... why y'all don't never know what y'all wanna eat though? That shit is crazy," he chuckled.

"What you wanna eat?" she fired back.

Mark's mind instantly went to the gutter, but he dismissed those thoughts.

"I actually got something in mind already because I knew yo ass was gon' hit me with the *it don't matter* line," he mimicked her.

"I was looking up restaurants on Lakeview, and it has some great reviews," Kash told him.

"Well I'll be damn... that's exactly where I was goin'," Mark admitted.

"Stop lying nigga."

"Real shit... they got some bomb ass shrimp and steak and I wanted you to try it. I just got a stop to make first."

"Hmph... you always tryna think like me and shit," Kash teased.

"Girl you be thinking like me... but it's all good, you learning from the best," he winked.

"No comment," Kash replied and pulled her phone out.

Mark turned into the cemetery a short while later. When Kash looked up and noticed where they were, she leaned over and put her hand on his leg. Mark had told her bits and pieces about his mom's death initially, but not much because it hurt him that he was away the past few years and then it was like she was gone within minutes. Kash wasn't having the silent treatment though. She made him open up completely and express his feelings and then she gave him the real deal. There were several reasons why Mark loved Kash so much and her being so supportive during one of the hardest times of his life was at the top of the list. His girlfriend Aiesha didn't give a damn about his feelings. That was the main reason he fucked Tasha, because he was hurt.

Mark got out and Kash was right by his side before he could take a step. She had grabbed the flowers from the back seat before he could do so. They made their way to his mother's resting place, and Mark stood there in silence. Kash had her arms wrapped around him and her presence was all that he needed in that exact moment. She handed him the flowers and Mark placed them on Michelle's grave.

"I know she's smiling down on all of you. She raised three wonderful kids."

The words Kash spoke made Mark smile. After a few more seconds, they were back in the car and on the way to *Hibachi Grill*. Mark shifted the mood by turning on some old school Jeezy. Jeezy was one of his top five rappers no matter what, and he could go to him at any given moment to lift his spirits. It took them almost thirty minutes to make it to the restaurant and secure a parking spot because how hectic traffic was. Mark vowed not to complain about Chicago's traffic because after being in New York for a couple of years, he saw firsthand that shit was worse there.

They made their way inside and were seated immediately. Mark and Kash both ordered Mountain Dew to drink when the waitress asked. The restaurant was semi-packed, but no one was seated directly by them, so Mark took that as an opportunity to discuss a little business.

"So, how you feeling about everything? You straight?"

"Yeah, I'm loving everything. I think I impressed Goo the other day with the shit I told you about, so I shouldn't have any more problems out of him," Kash jested.

"You and Goo getting pretty close I see," Mark hinted.

"It's all business... and look, speaking of the devil, this is him texting now," Kash said as she looked at her phone.

"He wants to meet up tonight at my crib, so he can show me how to do the counts," Kash continued.

Before Mark could reply, their drinks were placed in front of them and the waitress was ready to take their orders. They ordered their food and enjoyed their meals, but Mark couldn't help but to feel like shit with Goo and Kash was about to go left.

Chapter 20

Ebony sat on the edge of the bed and watched Kelsey and Melissa look through their shopping bags. She admired all the designer clothing they had and wished she had the guts to steal the shit like they did. When they invited her to the mall, she had no idea that she would become an accessory to a crime. The way they went into those stores, ripped off the censors, and stuffed the shit in their bags, in a matter of seconds, blew her mind. They even tossed her a few things in there, although she let them know from the beginning that she wasn't down with the shit. Ebony wasn't a spoiled little rich girl, but there wasn't *nothing* she wanted bad enough to steal. She wasn't judging them because they were her girls. She just knew for future references to decline any invitation that involved the mall.

"Ima put this on tonight so Goo can see me," Melissa said, prancing around the room with some black lace lingerie in hand.

"Girl, I told you that Goo ass wasn't going to be there tonight. They must have gotten into it bad this time because the nigga ain't been home in days," Ebony replied.

"DAYS!! Well that's good for me. If he ain't thinking about yo cousin, then I'm the one that can be on his mind," she stated.

Ebony caught the look that Kelsey gave her and wondered what it was about; however, she didn't have to wait long because Kelsey let it be known.

"Girl, you still got hopes on being with that man. It was a year or two ago and didn't you say it was a one-time thing?" Kelsey asked.

Melissa stopped dead in her tracks and cut Kelsey a dirty look.

"Regardless of how long ago it was, *BITCH*, I'm still his baby mother," she snapped.

"How? How Sway? He made you get an abortion and..."

"AND WHAT? You sound real pressed over there," Melissa interrupted her.

"If I'm pressed, then you crazy, need I remind you?" Kelsey shot back.

The two of them stood face to face, going back and forth. Ebony wasn't sure exactly what was going on. She kind of felt bad being as cool with Melissa as she was, seeing how she once slept with her cousin's man; but that was before her and she had nothing to do with it. She did know she was wrong for inviting them over tonight for Candy's ladies night, but she didn't want to be uncomfortable around Candy's friends, especially that bitch Micah. Ebony was shocked when Micah reached out to her regarding the sleepover. She said that Candy needed a night to let her hair down so Ebony agreed.

"Look y'all, I'm about to bounce... be at my crib by seven," Ebony said, getting up from the bed, heading to the car.

The both of them agreed and Ebony went on about her day. She hopped into Candy's BMW, cut the GPS on, and headed to the grocery store to get the last of the things for tonight. She stopped at Wal-Mart and grabbed a case of water, a few bags of chips, along with dip and other sweets like cookies and pies. After tackling those long lines, an hour later, she was headed back to the house. With traffic being on her side today, she pulled up in front of Candy's place in fifteen minutes. She killed the engine and reached in the backseat for her purse when her phone started ringing. Ebony's heart dropped when Brandon's name flashed across her screen. Brandon was her boyfriend back home, who had been extremely distant since she moved to Chicago. They had been together for the last year and a half and Ebony loved him to death, but he didn't treat her right. She had only spoken to him twice, and she had been in Chicago for almost a month. But regardless, she was always there at his ever beckon call.

"Hey baby," she sang happily in the phone.

"What's up?" he replied dryly, causing her face to frown.

"I miss you Brandon," she beamed.

"Couldn't miss me that much, you left me."

"I did not leave you. I didn't have a choice," she whined.

"Whatever man, look. I just wanted to holler at you about some shit. I fucked up and got myself in some shit that I can't get out of...." he stated.

"Oh my God Brandon, what? Are you ok?" she worried.

"I'm straight. Ima be straight. I gotta go dip out for a minute, which means you may not hear from me for a while. I'm going to try and reach out, but if months pass, then a nigga might be dead."

Hearing Brandon speak of death caused tears to flood her vision automatically.

"What is it? Any way I can help?" she inquired.

"Not unless you have ten-thousand dollars or some work, then I'm sure you can't."

Ebony knew exactly what Brandon was saying without him *actually* saying it. Brandon worked for one of the biggest drug dealers in Detroit name Scotty. Scotty was a ruthless motherfucker who cared about nothing but his money. Ebony was sure that Brandon must have gotten into shit involving him and now his life was on the line.

"Just come to Chicago," she begged.

"To Chicago for what? That nigga will find me there," he replied.

"What if I told you that I had access to that amount of money and that type of work?" she stated.

"Then I swear to God, *if* you make that happen, then I'll make you *my wife*," he replied.

Ebony rested her head on the headrest inside the car. There was nothing in the world she wouldn't do for Brandon, even if that meant stealing from her own cousin. She knew Goo had bread. She just didn't know how much but from the lifestyle they were living, Ray Charles could see that they were well off. The wheels in her head began to turn. She had to find a way to get her hands on that money for her man, and she knew just where to start. She ended the call with him, promising that she'll come through before getting out the car. She went around and grabbed the bags out of the trunk before heading up the stairs into the house. As soon as she opened the door, she bumped into Goo. He must have been in big ass hurry to leave before Candy got there because he dropped a wad of money and never looked back. Ebony felt like it must have been her lucky day because she picked the shit up, hurried to her room, and called Brandon right back.

Chapter 21

It had been two days since Candy had last seen Goo. She hadn't called him, and he hadn't bothered to call her. She knew that he had been by the house because things were out of place, which meant that he was purposely avoiding her. Candy felt so conflicted. She was pissed the fuck off at Goo, but it wasn't like she could just turn her love off for him like a light switch. It was finally Friday and Candy was actually a little ready for the kickback that Micah had planned. The day after the breakup, Candy missed work for the first time since she had been on maternity leave or anything resulting around her son. Her mom's motherly instincts must have kicked in because she called that morning with a voice full of concern. Within that next hour, she had convinced Candy that she was on her way back to Chicago. After fussing with her mom the day before and losing the battle, Candy allowed RJ to go back to Michigan for a week or two while she got herself together, as her mom instructed. It was a very hard decision, but Candy knew that RJ would be in great hands with her mom.

Since Candy didn't have any appointments that day, she caught up on research until noon and then left and went to the salon. Her girl had her down for a twelve thirty appointment. Candy hadn't had much of an appetite, so she grabbed a bottle of water out of her mini fridge and some nabs out of the vending machine on her way out. Twenty minutes later, she pulled up to the beauty salon, parked, and got out. Candy always loved the place because the atmosphere was pleasant and very relaxing. The waterfalls to the left when you walked in the door wer so soothing. Kajara's chair was waiting on her, just as she expected because she was a stylist that didn't overbook. She didn't believe in having people waiting in the salon all day and night to get their hair down. To her, it was unprofessional and Candy couldn't agree with her more.

"Heeyyy boo… your girl Micah just left about ten minutes ago," Kajara said as she sat down in the chair.

"I forgot she said she had an appointment today. We supposed to be getting together later tonight," Candy replied as her beautician began combing through her hair.

"She invited me, but I'm working late tonight. You know how the weekends go."

"Yeah, you stay busy… make that money though."

"So, what you getting today?" Jara quizzed.

Candy paused for a second. She honestly didn't know what she wanted, but she knew that she wanted something different. The situation with Goo had her emotions all over the damn place.

"I'm feeling like Angela Bassett in *Waiting To Exhale* today," Candy finally admitted.

"Whaattt? What the hell going on with you?" Jara spun her chair around and asked.

Candy sighed and gave Jara the simplified version of her problems. She started with the incident about RJ because it still bothered her. Candy was thankful that her baby was okay, but she was still conflicted. Her mom taking him would probably work out for the best and allow her to clear her mind. She later told her about Goo and the last argument that they had. Surprisingly, Jara took Goo's side and told Candy that he was the type that you stay on because his head was so deep in the streets. Candy didn't expect Jara to take up for Goo, but as she listened, she actually made some valid points. It wasn't enough for Candy to break down and call Goo, but she did let what her beautician said sink in.

By the time Jara was done, she didn't even cut Candy's hair. She told her that she didn't want her making any drastic changes like that while she wasn't thinking clearly. However, she did give her a completely different look. Since Candy pretty much always wore her natural hair, she looked different with the bundles of Brazilian deep wave hair that Jara had installed. Candy was impressed when she looked in the mirror, and she couldn't help but to tip her girl for coming through like she always did.

"Goo ain't gon' be able to keep his hands off you," Jara beamed.

"Girl… I'll just keep my comment to myself. Let me go on the nail shop and get these hands and feet taken care of. See ya later boo," Candy waved.

Candy left the salon and made her way to get her mani and pedi. It was crowded because it was Friday, but her loyalty and good tipping afforded her the privilege of not having to wait in line. She walked out of the shop an hour and fifteen minutes later. Candy called her mom during commute home and checked up on RJ. He was doing fine just as expected and then Candy talked to her dad the rest of the ride home. By the time she made it home, it was right at five o'clock. Micah told her that she would be there between five and five thirty to setup everything. As far as Candy knew, it was going to be a night of food, music, and drinks, and Candy was more than ready for a few drinks.

A few minutes later, Candy's phone rang, and it was Micah letting her know that she was outside. Candy finished changing into an Adidas jogger and shoes really quick and then went outside and helped Micah gather stuff. She smelled Goo's Versace cologne lingering and knew that he had been there again. Candy sighed and then hurriedly made her way back outside.

"Girl... what all you got. It ain't but three of us right?"

"I told your cousin to invite one of her friends... didn't want her to feel left out, ya know," Micah told her as she grabbed some bags.

They loaded up both of their arms and made two trips before they had everything that Micah had bought. Most of it was liquor and Candy wasn't mad.

"You making margaritas?" she quizzed as she held up a big ass bottle of *Jose Cuervo*.

"Texas Margaritas... I found a recipe online and the shit gotta be banging."

Candy smelled pizza and her stomach actually started growling. She grabbed a slice of sausage pizza and smashed it.

"You haven't been eating I see... well eat up because we're definitely going to drink up.

A few minutes later, Ebony appeared in the living room.

"I didn't even know you were here. You didn't hear me come in?" Candy asked.

"I was taking a nap, but my girls just called and said they are right around the corner, so I got up."

Candy continued eating the other slice of pizza and wings that she put on a plate while Micah was in the kitchen about to prepare drinks. She heard the blender start around the same time she heard Ebony squealing and speaking to whoever she had invited. Ebony walked back with two girls following close behind her. They all made introductions after Micah appeared and Candy learned that the girls names were Melissa and Kelsey. Ebony connected her phone to the Bluetooth speaker and *Boo'd Up* by Ella Mai filled the house. All of the girls sang to the top of their lungs, and by the time the song was over, everyone appeared to be in a good mood. Candy felt like it was about to be a great night.

Micah made everyone a drink and sat them down in front of them. Once they were done eating, they shifted to the living room with their drinks and lounged while talking shit about men.

"If I had a man like Goo... I would be happy all the time," Melissa said, and Candy didn't miss the look that Ebony and Kelsey gave her. Apparently, Micah didn't either because she cleared her throat and gave Candy a look that said "*I might have to hurt these bitches.*" Candy bit her tongue, but she was feeling the exact same way.

"Let's take some shots," Ebony jested as she got up and grabbed the liquor and shot glasses that Micah had set out.

"Oooh let's make it fun. Let's play *never have I ever...* y'all know how that goes right?" Kelsey quizzed and everyone nodded their heads.

"I'll start... never have I ever gave head," Candy said, and everyone laughed and took their shot because they all knew that she was just ready to drink.

"Okay... I'm next I guess. Never have I ever fucked somebody else's man," Micah said, and Candy knew that her friend was just trying to get a feel of the girls in the room.

It dawned on her that Goo belonged to someone else after she saw everyone take a shot, except for Micah. Candy went ahead and took hers and Ebony gasped.

"Coussiinnn... let me find out you be out there living and shit."

"Girl... it was unintentional, but it happened so it is what it is."

"If you say so... your turn Kelsey," Ebony nudged her.

"Never have I ever got pregnant by somebody else's man and was forced to get an abortion."

Candy's eyes bucked as Melissa smirked and took a shot.

"Maybe we shouldn't have started this game. This shit gets personal," Ebony gasped.

"Shit happens," Melissa shrugged.

Candy began to get a bad vibe all of a sudden. The way that Micah was looking at the girls, she must have felt the same way.

"Y'all got something y'all wanna say?" Micah stood up and asked.

"It's just a game damn," Ebony fumed.

Just like that, the cordialness that her friend and cousin had been displaying was gone out of the window. Candy stood up and pulled Micah into the kitchen.

"I ain't feeling these hoes," Micah confirmed her thoughts before she even had the chance to speak on it.

"I ain't gon' lie... something ain't right, but let's make the best of this night that you put together."

They chatted for a few more minutes and then headed back to the living room. Candy heard the front door open, and she knew that it had to be Goo because the door was locked.

"Hey," he spoke when he they locked eyes, causing Candy to speak back and then, she saw Malik right behind him.

"Where RJ?"

"With my mom," she replied.

Candy heard some whispering amongst Ebony and her friends and she saw how Ebony was staring at Malik. It was a good thing that

Micah's back was turned to her. Goo walked off in a hurry like he was looking for something. A few seconds later, he came back and asked her if she had saw some money that he may have dropped.

"Nah."

"Ask your cousin. She was walking in when I left earlier."

Candy called Ebony over and asked her if she found anything, and Ebony looked away and told her *no*. Her body language was all off, but before Candy could ask her anything else, Ebony had rejoined her friends.

"Hey Malik... you not speaking today?" Ebony said out of nowhere.

"Oh... wassup ladies. Did you enjoy the club?" Malik inquired.

"Hell yeah... we'll be back... for more reasons than one," Ebony tried to mumble the last part, but Candy heard her loud and clear, and she knew Micah did too.

"Aight... we out," Goo said.

Malik said goodbye to everyone and then kissed Micah before he left. The look on Ebony's face was one that was mixed with jealousy and anger. Candy made a mental note to talk to her little cousin before she messed around and got fucked up by Micah.

Chapter 22

"Hello," Mark answered with a voice full of annoyance because he already knew who was calling.

"Why you keep ignoring me?" Aiesha whined.

"What the fuck you mean? What we got to talk about?"

"I miss you, baby. You don't miss me?"

"Nah, I'm good on you. I told you it was over, and I don't understand why you can't get that through your fuckin' head."

"I'm pregnant, Mark."

"The fuck you telling me for? I can't even have kids. I got a vasectomy when I turned eighteen," he lied.

The silence on the other end of the phone let him know that Aiesha was lying and was still full of shit. She couldn't think of a quick enough comeback, so Mark hung up. He didn't do the blocking shit, but it was looking like he might have to start because Aiesha had been getting on his motherfuckin' nerves. Mark turned into one of the spots and parked. Malik sent him to check on some shit and pick up some money since he was handling some business with Goo and Goo couldn't do it. An eerie feeling came over Mark, so he sat there for a minute. By instinct, he put the car back into gear and pulled away. A few seconds later, shots rang out and Mark pressed the gas pedal to the floor. A bullet hit the back window, and it shattered instantly. Mark ducked down and got the hell away from there.

Mark didn't feel like that was a part of the other shit that was going on because he was meeting up with a worker, but he knew that niggas switched up every day, so it could have been. He shot Malik a text and let him know that he had an emergency. Malik texted right back and told him to meet him at the club. Mark made his way to Club Escape and parked in the back. It was a little after ten when he pulled up, but Mark decided to go inside and grab a drink. He knew that he had at least fifteen minutes to spare. He made his way inside and the club was packed, which was normal for a Friday night. After flirting with the bartender and tossing back three shots, Mark felt his phone vibrate. It was Malik letting him know that him and Goo were upstairs.

Mark made his way and when he walked in, he could tell that the both of them had shit on their minds.

"What happened?" Malik wasted no time asking.

Mark ran everything down to them and they listened. He let them know that no one chased him and that made it seem like someone may have been after Goo since he was supposed to be the one who was meeting someone there.

"I'll handle that shit," Goo said and confirmed Mark's thoughts.

"What yo ass done did now? You know what… I don't even wanna know man. Just fix the shit because we have enough bullshit goin' on already," Malik stated.

"I got it… that lil bitch. Listen, Ima go do the count wit' ol' girl and then Ima chill out. I gotta get some shit straight," Goo said and bounced.

Mark knew exactly where Goo was going, but it was, so he kept his mouth closed. Malik started talking to him about his MOM program and what he wanted to do for Mother's Day, and Mark loved the ideas that he had in mind. They talked for about another thirty until Malik was called downstairs to handle a situation in the club. Mark decided to go on home. It had been a long ass day and the next day was going to pretty much be the same.

Instead of going to his new place, Mark decided to head home. Home would always be the pace his parents made for them no matter what. When he made it, Mesha was out with her boyfriend, so Mark chopped it up with his dad before he headed upstairs and took a shower. His little super head had texted him by the time he got out of the shower, but Mark didn't bother hitting her back up. He decided to save her for the next night. Her head was banging, but Mark wasn't going to give her the satisfaction of thinking that she had him wrapped around her finger. That little *what's up* text would have led to more if he would have answered.

The next morning, Mark expected to wake up to the smell of bacon and eggs or something, but after he got dressed, he saw that Mesha never came in. Luck just wasn't on his side because he had planned on eating good before getting her to run him downtown to handle some business. Going downtown alone wasn't going to work. He needed someone to stay in the car while he went inside. Mark texted Micah to see what she was doing and told her that he needed her to ride with him in about twenty minutes. She texted back and told him to pick her up from Candy's house.

Thirty minutes later, he pulled up and called his sister. Micah walked out with Candy right behind her. Candy was beautiful. Mark could tell why Goo was going crazy over whatever they had going on. He didn't know the details of the situation, but it was clear that they were on bad terms.

"Hey big head… we were planning on going out for breakfast, so we decided we would both just roll with you after you texted."

"Aight bet," Mark replied and backed out.

"Shit… I forgot to get that damn paper," Mark mumbled and made a quick detour.

Micah had connected her iPhone and her and Candy started rapping along with Cardi B. Mark didn't know which song they were listening to. All he knew that both of them were singing off key about someone not hitting their line anymore. He shrugged both of them off and parked when he made it to his destination, parked, and got out.

"Wait… I gotta pee," Micah told him and got out.

"Didn't you just leave the house girl?" he fussed.

By the time he got to the door, Mark reached into his pocket, but realized that he didn't have his key, so he knocked. He heard Micah say something to Candy just as the door opened.

"Hey… I need that manila folder, so I can go turn the paperwork in," Mark spoke.

"Oh yeah… okay let me grab it."

"Can I use your bathroom sis?" Micah chimed in.

Kash ushered them in and closed the door.

"Come on Micah, you can use the bathroom that's in my room."

Mark watched as Micah followed Kash, but before they could exit the living room, Goo appeared wearing some shorts and no shoes or socks. Mark followed Goo's eyes straight to Candy's, and he knew that all hell was about to break loose.

Chapter 23

In the past, Goo had cheated more times than he could count, yet he had never been caught red-handed. The crazy thing was, he looked guilty as fuck at that very moment, but nothing happened. Outside of getting his dick sucked by one of his workers, he hadn't done anything at all. The night before, he stopped by Kash's crib to show her how to do the count. They talked about everything under the sun, including the issues Goo and Candy had been having. After smoking about four blunts and drinking a fifth of *Hennessey*, they passed out on the couch. Kash's heat must have been on hell because Goo was sweating bullets, which was the reason he was shirtless. The situation looked all bad, but in all truthfulness, it was innocent.

"The fuck y'all got going on here?" Mark barked, looking back and forth between Kash and Goo like he wanted to kill them both.

"Look, it's not how it looks," Goo spoke up first.

"Bullshit! It looks like you were caught fucking this bitch," Candy screamed.

"Look ma, I know you upset, but the name calling gotta chill," Kash replied as respectful as she could.

"You not in a position to tell my friend what the fuck to do, seeing how you in here with *HER* man," Micah stepped in.

"Regardless of who man is who, this is *my* motherfucking house," Kash snapped.

"Aye! Aye! Aye! Everybody chill the fuck out. Kash and I...." Goo began to speak but was cut off by Candy.

"Wait... so this is Kash? The *same* Kash you referred to as *Mark homie,* but you failed to mention that Kash had a pussy," Candy snapped.

"Mannnnn... Candy you doing too fuckn' much right now," Goo replied, tossing on his Nike shirt.

"I'm doing too much? I walk in on my man in *another* bitch house, and you have the nerve to say *I'm* doing too much," Candy yelled.

"Look, I tried to be as nice as possible, but y'all gotta get the fuck outta my crib! Mark, *I ain't fuck Goo*, and Candy, *Goo ain't fuck me*! But the disrespect has to stop because at this point, I don't *give a fuck* who is who... if I'm disrespected again, I'm fucking some shit up," Kash explained.

"No disrespect to you, but you gotta understand where she's coming from," Micah added in.

"But I do, and like we've both stated, nothing happened. After last night, I look at Goo like a big brother. The nigga fell asleep on the couch after talking my ears off about you Candy," Kash let it be known.

For the first time, everyone in the room was quiet. Goo looked around at them before tossing on his coat.

"First, I prepared to propose and that didn't work out. Next, you walk in on some shit but instead of asking questions, you wanna cut up. Not only do you *sound* stupid, you *look* stupid as well. I'm moving *all* my shit out and I hope you, and that fuck boy be happy together," Goo said as he brushed pass Candy and out of the door.

Goo reached the elevator and pressed the down button. As soon as the doors opened, Mark called out to him. As bad as he wanted to say *fuck Mark* too and bounce, he couldn't. Mark was his boy and they needed to talk.

"You good?" an out of breath Mark asked as he jogged down the long hallway.

"Yeah, I'm straight," Goo lied.

"Mannnn look, you and Candy need to handle that situation. It did look bad my nigga," Mark explained.

"Yeah it may have looked that way, but my word should be bond. If I say ain't shit happen, then ain't shit happen."

"Nigga, you act like you got the best track record when it comes to cheating," Mark reminded him.

Goo couldn't help but laugh because his homie was right. All the shit from his past was biting him in the ass, the one time he *wanted* to do right.

"Listen, y'all need to talk and make this shit work," Mark stated, but truthfully, Goo wasn't trying to hear it. He was fed up with the bullshit that came with being in a relationship.

"Aight I hear you bruh, but since you are giving advice and shit, Kash loves you nigga. You need to work on that," Goo replied before entering the elevator.

He took the elevator to the first floor and headed to his car. He planned on grabbing his shit like he threatened and move it to his condo downtown. As he drove, he thought about his son and how much he loved waking up to him every morning. Goo grew up without a father, and after his mother was killed by her bitch ass boyfriend Pimp, Goo was left without a family. Ever since the day RJ was born, he vowed to always be in his life no matter what, but the shit him and Candy was dealing with made him feel like co-parenting may be the best thing. With all the arguing and shit from that morning, Goo hadn't even realized he hadn't ate anything since the day before until his stomach began to growl. With all the liquor he consumed, he knew that he needed to eat something quick or things would be all bad. He got off the expressway at Independence and made a sharp right into the parking lot of *Maxwell's*. *Maxwell's* was a twenty-four hour polish stand that was cracking regardless of the time. It was most people's go to spot to sober up after the club, and Goo couldn't wait to get him a deep fried polish with extra onions. He double parked his car and hopped out. There were about three people ahead of him. He blew his breath into his hands, trying to warm up while he waited. The best thing about the place was their quickness. They got you in and out in a matter of seconds. After the few people ahead of him grabbed their greasy brown paper bags, Goo stepped up to the window.

"Goo... Buddy!" Ahmed, the owner, greeted him.

"What up my nigga? Let me get... ummmmmm... a deep-fried polish, extra grilled onions and no peppers," he requested.

As Ahmed began to prepare his food, Goo pulled his phone from his pocket to check his messages. Noticing nothing of importance, he placed it back in his coat just as Ahmed handed him the bag. Goo pulled a wad of cash from his jeans, piled off a ten, placed it on the counter, and turned to walk away; but, he collided with the person behind him.

"My bad big homie," Goo apologized, never really looking at the gentleman.

"Yeah, I know yo bad...*BITCH!*" the male's voice echoed through Goo's ears as he continued to walk away.

Goo stopped in his tracks and turned around, only to find a brave James walking towards him.

"Niggaz walk around like they God, like they can't be touched," James uttered.

"Bitch... *I'm* yo GOD," Goo laughed as he tossed a fry from the bag into his mouth.

"You think this shit a game? You think you can just fuck my wife in *my* house and dip out like there would be no consequences?" he asked with a straight face.

Goo tilted his head to the side and laughed again before grabbing his pistol from his waist and shooting James in the head.

"Now, you don't have to worry about *nobody* fucking yo bitch," Goo spat before walking off.

He jumped in his car and peeled off, ignoring the screams from the patrons around him. He knew that he could have handled that situation differently, but dude ass was popping off at the mouth too much. With all the enemies they had floating around in the streets, there was no time to spare any lives. Why wait until tomorrow to handle some shit that could be taken care of today?

Before Goo could reach the end of the block, his cell phone rang.

"Yeah?" he answered on the second ring.

"I took the cameras down and made sure the people that was out there does not talk," the caller informed him.

"Good looking Ahmed, I owe you big time," Goo replied.

"No problem boss," he stated before ending the call.

Whether James was or wasn't one of those niggaz plotting against Goo and his team will forever be unknown, but it didn't matter to Goo either way. James was one less fuck nigga in Chicago he had to deal with. Goo connected his phone to the car charger and headed to the crib him and Candy shared, one last time.

Chapter 24

Ebony stood quietly by Candy's bedroom door and eavesdropped while she gossiped on the phone. From what she was hearing, it seemed like Goo had been caught fucking some chick. Hearing the news didn't surprise Ebony because Goo and Candy was like night and day. She didn't understand how they got wrapped up in the first place, but the words that Candy spoke next answered her question.

"I blame myself. I should have known because I was his side bitch. The fuck was I thinking; *like* that nigga was going to upgrade me to wifey status. Once a dog ass niggaz, always one," she snapped.

Ebony used her right hand to cover her mouth because she felt herself about to scream. She couldn't believe her ears, but what Candy said next was the icing on the cake.

"Here I am, an attorney, and I'm fucking with one of the most notorious drug lords in Chicago. I'm risking it all for a nigga who won't risk shit for me," she stated.

Ebony began to tip toe backward until she reached her room. Once inside, she closed the door, making sure to lock it just in case someone forgot the knock. She went over to the bed where she snatched up her phone to call Brandon, but she noticed she already had three missed calls from him, so she dialed him back immediately.

"Why the fuck you not answering your phone?" he practically screamed in her ear.

"I'm sorry... I was being nosey, but I was just about to call you. I know for a fact we can get you that money so you can repay Scotty and be good," she replied excitedly.

"That's good to hear, but I really need for you to do is open the front door."

"Open the front door? For what? What front door?" she asked confused.

"Man is you slow? You told me to come to Chicago the last time we spoke, so I did. Why you think a nigga asked for the address?" he inquired.

"I thought maybe you wanted the address to send me something. I had no idea you was coming," she explained.

"Look man, open the fucking door, its cold out here," he yelled before ending the call.

Ebony sat on the bed lost. Why the fuck wouldn't he tell her he was coming? She couldn't just pop up with a nigga at Candy's house. The sound of her phone ringing caused her to jump. She looked down to see Brandon calling again. Instead of answering it, she jumped up, grabbed her hoodie out the closet, and went to the front door. As soon as she stepped out, the cold March air smacked her in the face. She looked around for a few seconds before noticing Brandon walking down the street towards the house. She quickly skipped down the stairs and walked towards his direction to meet him. A smile as big as the Grinch invaded her face as she watched his 6'2 skinny frame walk towards her. Unable to control herself, she jogged the rest of the way and jumped into his arms. Ebony wrapped her small arms around his neck, kissing his face as he gripped her ass. After the public display of affection was completed, he placed her on the ground, and they slowly walked back towards the house.

"I know these motherfuckers got money, look at this neighborhood," Brandon stated, admiring the scenery around him.

"Yeah they do, and I just found out that the nigga Goo is sum like a drug lord," she bragged.

"Did you say Goo?" he stopped and asked.

"Yeah why?" she quizzed.

"Mannnn… the whole Midwest know about him and his homie Malik. They like the gods of the drug world. Why the fuck you ain't mention his name sooner?" he questioned.

"I thought I did," she hunched her shoulders.

"If I can get my hands on the type of money they touching, a nigga will never have to work again a day in his life," Brandon canted.

Instead of replying, Ebony just shook her head in agreement as she tried to think of ways to make that happen.

"Goo not to be fucked with, but neither am I. Plus my back against the wall, I gotta do what I gotta do," he continued.

"Listen to me, it will be easy," she promised as she grabbed his face, forcing him to look into her eyes.

"How much did you say he dropped and left behind?" Brandon inquired.

"That was only four thousand, but it gets us closer to how much you owe Scotty. And besides, that's chump change to Goo. He ain't missing that shit."

"Aight bet. I need you to find out all you can about where that nigga keeps his money. I know for a fact that there is a safe somewhere in the crib. I gotta give dude ass his money in two weeks, so this *needs* to happen ASAP."

Ebony stood there and wondered if she could actually pull it off. Brandon was right. There had to be a safe somewhere, the hard part was figuring out where exactly it was. Ebony reflected back to the conversation she overheard and wondered if the fact that Goo and Candy was on bad terms would help or hinder her plans. She had some serious thinking to do, but right then, her mind was somewhere else.

"Where you staying?"

"I'm staying here with you," he answered quickly.

"*No the fuck you not! I'm* barely staying here. Candy and Goo will have a fit," she panicked.

Brandon began to laugh, "I'm just bullshitting. I got a hotel not too far from here. Go grab your shit. I need some of that pussy ASAP!" he said, followed by a smack on her ass.

Ebony wasted no time running back down to the house to pack an overnight bag. She had been manless, which resulted into being dickless since she been in Chicago. The thought of getting some dick alone made her pussy wet. When she entered the house, Candy was now sitting on the couch watching TV.

"I didn't even know you left," Candy stated, looking up briefly from the *The Haves and Have Nots*.

"My bad, I was only outside. My boyfriend came to visit me from Michigan," she beamed.

"Awwww shit! I didn't know you was in a relationship. Well, where he at? Tell him he can come in," Candy replied.

Ebony stood there for a second contemplating on whether or not she should take Candy up on her offer. She didn't want to seem suspicious by declining, so she grabbed her phone from her pocket and sent Brandon a text.

Ebony: My cousin wants to meet you. Come in for a second so shit won't look crazy.

Brandon: Bet

Ebony watched a commercial or two while they waited on Brandon. About two minutes later, the doorbell rang. Candy paused the TV and turned to the door while Ebony went to answer it. Ebony and her boyfriend walked into the front room where Ebony introduced the two.

"Candy, this is my baby Brandon. Brandon, this is my favorite cousin Candy," Ebony lied.

"Well, it's nice to meet you," Candy stood from the couch and shook his hand before returning back to her spot.

"Nice to meet you too ma'am," Brandon replied in the fakest proper accent ever, causing Ebony to giggle.

"He's handsome girl…. So, what you two got planned?" Candy asked.

"Nothing much. I'm about to chill with him. He got a room at a hotel nearby," Ebony spoke up first.

"Cool, well I'm not going to hold y'all long. Have fun."

The couple both said their goodbyes to Candy and prepared to leave when the front door opened. Goo walked in with a sleeping RJ in his arms. He eyeballed Brandon before walking pass everyone else without saying a word. He placed RJ in his room and then returned back to the living room.

"I really think you should give up your key since you no longer reside here," Candy said from the sofa.

"I pay this mortgage and my son lay his head here. Therefore, if you want shit to change, then you better change those locks," Goo replied, walking back out the door.

Ebony eyes landed on Candy's, who was clearly embarrassed and ready to curse him out, but it was too late. Just as quick as he appeared, he disappeared. Candy snatched her phone off the couch and headed upstairs to her room. Once she was out of sight, Brandon turned and looked at Ebony.

"These motherfuckers don't look like a happy family to me."

"Yeah me either but that might work in our favor. Come on, I got an idea."

Chapter 25

It had been a week since the incident that happened at Kash's place, and things between Goo and Candy were still the same. He walked in and dropped RJ off and dipped right back out, the same as he had done the day before. Before Candy left Kash's crib, Kash actually stopped her and told her that everything was really innocent. Candy believed her and even apologized for calling her a bitch, but she never addressed anything with Goo. Kissing his ass wasn't an option. No matter how Goo tried to flip the shit on her, it still wasn't right. In Candy's eyes, he should have never put himself in that type of situation. To add insult to injury, he had just embarrassed her in front of her cousin and her boyfriend. It wasn't that Candy was one to put on a front, but honestly, she didn't know that nigga with her cousin and the least Goo could have did was stayed until they left. Since he wanted to continue acting a fool, Candy was over playing the good girl role.

"What a pleasant surprise!" Lorenzo said after answering the phone after the second ring.

"I know... I'm surprised you answered, but I'm glad you did," Candy nervously replied.

"You know you always have a friend in me."

"I need to talk to you... as friends. I need a male's point of view."

"I got you... you wanna meet up?"

"Yeah... what about tomorrow?" Candy quizzed.

"I'm free tomorrow night. How about you meet me at *Morton's Steakhouse*? I heard the food there is delicious," Lorenzo offered.

Candy paused for a minute. That was her favorite restaurant, but her last memory there wasn't one that she wanted to relive. After a few moments of silence, she finally agreed to meet Lorenzo the next night at seven after letting him know that it really wasn't a date. After Candy hung up, she finished up her glass of wine and then went and checked on RJ. He was sleeping peacefully in his crib, so Candy went to her room, stripped out of her clothes, hopped in bed, and then reached into the nightstand and grabbed her bullet. Since she wasn't being fucked on the regular like she was used to, something had to give. It only took about two minutes for her to bust a nut and then she drifted off to sleep.

The next morning, Candy woke up to the sound of RJ laughing on the baby monitor. She was glad that he wasn't a crybaby. Candy got up and noticed that it was still early as hell. It was only a quarter after seven, but RJ had slept all night, so it was time for him to get up. She walked into the room and bumped into Goo.

"Good morning," he surprised her and spoke.

"Good morning," Candy spoke back.

"Hey mommy's baby," she smiled at her son, and he reached for her.

"Oh so that's how it is lil man... I was the one in here when yo lil ass woke up," Goo joked.

Candy felt RJ's pamper.

"I already changed him," Goo stated.

"Oh... well let's go get some breakfast," Candy tickled RJ and headed for the door.

"We need to talk," Goo grabbed her arm and said before she made it to the door.

Just the touch of his hand made Candy's knees weak. No matter how hard she tried to be, she missed the hell out of Goo. Candy sighed because she knew that he was right. She told herself to try and stay calm, especially in front of their son.

"I agree," Candy finally sighed.

She continued walking towards the kitchen so that she could feed RJ. He loved oatmeal, so she mentally decided that she would make him some before she reached the kitchen. Candy had a lot that she wanted to say, but she was going to let Goo talk first since he was the one who initiated the conversation. Candy placed RJ in his high chair and then went to make some oatmeal.

"No matter what happens between us, I'll always be here for my son. I don't want another nigga raising my son."

"So, is this an official break up?" Candy put her hands on her hips.

"Clearly, I ain't good at this relationship shit. I been tryna do right, but my right ain't good enough. I can't be the man that you really want, but I'll be the best father that I can be to my son."

"Wow," was all that Candy could say.

She felt tears threatening to fall, but she tried her best to suck them up. Goo's choice of words was not what she expected at all. Candy thought that he was ready to work their relationship out, but he threw her for a loop.

"Maybe some time apart will help us.... *shit*, I don't know. I just know I can't deal wit' us arguing all the damn time," Goo shrugged.

"I agree," Candy managed to say.

There was an awkward silence. Candy forced herself to finish fixing RJ's food and then she handed it to Goo. She couldn't stand to look at him anymore because she knew her tears were about to fall soon. Candy handed Goo the oatmeal so that he could feed RJ, and she went to the bathroom. After turning on the shower, Candy stepped in and cried until she couldn't cry anymore. She thought about all of things that she had gone through with Goo. There was actually more good than bad, but she wasn't one to beg and maybe he was right. Time apart could either make them or break them. Candy stayed in the shower until the water began to cool down, and then she finally got out. She turned on the water to brush her teeth and then Goo called her name.

"Yeah?" Candy replied after a few seconds.

"RJ in the play pen. I'm out."

"Okay."

Candy knew that she was going to need strength to get through the break, breakup, or whatever it was, and she planned on keeping her meeting with Lorenzo just to start the process.

***

"Are you sure about this?" Micah asked as Candy brushed through her inches.

"We're just friends," Candy replied.

"Candy, you have on a *freakum* dress. You're going on a date! You can cut the friend shit out."

"Miccaahhhh… this isn't a date. I clarified that, but even if it was… I'm single remember. Goo made it clear this morning. Now are you going to keep fussing about me going out or are you going to watch RJ?"

"I wouldn't be here if I wasn't going to watch RJ, but I still think this date is a bad idea."

"Girl… I'll be back in a couple hours. You know to make yourself at home," Candy kissed RJ and headed out.

Micah had been trying to talk her out of meeting with Lorenzo ever since she called and asked her to babysit earlier. Candy normally listened to her girl, but she let those particular words go into one ear and out of the other. Thirty minutes later, Candy pulled up to the restaurant and parked. She freshened up her lip gloss and then got out. Brief thoughts of her last time there with Goo flashed into Candy's mind, but she quickly dismissed the thoughts. She told herself that Goo didn't want her, and she wasn't doing anything wrong. Candy's phone vibrated as soon as she walked inside the restaurant. It was a text from Lorenzo telling her that he had a table near the back. She spotted him midway there and right before she made it to the table, Lorenzo got up. They embraced and Candy inhaled his cologne and couldn't help but to think about Goo. *Maybe Micah was right. This is a bad idea,* Candy thought to herself. They let each other go, and he pulled her chair out and helped her get seated.

"I'm not sure what made you call, but I'm glad you did. You've changed Candy. I thought you were fine back then, but you're beyond beautiful," Lorenzo smiled and Candy blushed.

"Thank you. You don't look too bad yourself," Candy beamed.

The waitress took their drink and appetizer orders, and as soon as she left, Candy began talking to Lorenzo about life. She didn't dive right into her relationship problems. She allowed him to talk first. Once he asked her about herself, she opened up to him and told him all about Goo. It was crazy how easy it was for her to talk to Lorenzo, it was as if the friendship they had never missed a beat. Lorenzo wasn't the hating type. He told Candy to be honest with herself, and if Goo was who she wanted, then she needed to make it work. She listened and understood where he was coming from. It was the same thing that both Micah and Jara had told her.

The waitress brought their appetizers and placed them in front of them. They ordered their entrées and she walked off again. Candy made up her mind that she was going to have a real talk with Goo, one that she initiated and let him know the real deal. Life was too short to be playing games and neither of them were getting any younger. For the first time in weeks, Candy smiled. That smile was short lived when she looked up and saw Goo helping a woman into her seat directly across from her. His back was turned, but she knew that nigga in her sleep. The way the woman smiled up at him had Candy ready to catch a case right then and there.

Chapter 26

Out of all the places Tisha wanted to eat at, why the fuck did she have to choose *Morton's Steakhouse*? The last memories Goo had there wasn't a pleasant one, but he figured since she was doing him a favor, why not allow her pick where she wanted to dine?

"It's been a long time Rico. I can tell nothing much has changed," Tisha stated, looking over at Goo as she broke off a piece of bread.

"Well... a lot has changed," he laughed, looking down at the imprint of his dick.

Tisha must have caught on because her eyes followed his, but she redirected her attention quickly. But it was too late, Goo had already peeped it.

"How's Malik and the rest of the gang?" she asked, changing the subject.

"Everybody is good. Malik just got married," Goo advised her.

"Oh shit! Straight up? I always knew he would be the one to settle down. Tell him I said congratulations," she smiled.

"How about you tell him yourself at the grand opening of *RJ's World*," Goo stated.

"I am so proud of you Rico, like all bullshit aside. This fundraiser and the opening of *RJ's World* is some really dope shit. I'm glad me and my team can be a part of it," she beamed.

"I'm glad you agreed to help out Tisha. Without you, a lot of this wouldn't be possible," Goo advised her.

"Well look, it's done and we good to go. Now since you offered to take me out to show your gratitude, I'm about to order up some shit," she joked as she cracked opened the menu.

The two of them sat silently looking over things before Goo felt the presence of the waiter. He looked up from his menu, ready to place his order when he locked eyes with Candy, who stood in front of them with her hands on her hip. Goo ran his hands over his beard and shook his head. He was starting to think she put a GPS tracker or some shit in his ride because she was always popping up.

"So is this why you wanted to take a break?" she asked, her eyes darting back and forth between Tisha and Goo's.

"Candy, this is my friend Tisha. We grew up together. Tisha, this is RJ's mom," Goo introduced the two.

"Ohhh ok. How are you doing Candy? I've heard nothing but great things about you," Tisha replied, extending her hand for a handshake but Candy left her hanging.

"So, this what you do now? You tell yo hoes about me, so just in case you get caught, they can act like y'all real friends?" Candy asked.

"Look, you got the wrong impression. I'm just helping......"

Goo cut Tisha off. "*You* don't have to explain *shit*, I got this. Tisha is an old friend from the neighborhood, who just so happens to be an on-air radio personality. She's been helping me come up with ways to get exposure for the new organization I have, *RJ's World*. I planned on revealing it to you as well as our son on his first birthday."

Candy eyes went from an angry black woman to Mother Theresa's in a matter of seconds. Goo couldn't help but smirk. He loved the fuck out of Candy and knew that he was to blame for her insecurities.

"I am so sorry," Candy face turned red from embarrassment.

"Girl, no need to. Trust I understand," Tisha smiled.

"Ok, I'll let you to get back to work. Rico call me when you leave. I really wanna talk to you," Candy requested before turning to leave.

Goo looked at Tisha, who stared at him and smiled.

"So, that's her."

"That's my baby!" Goo said with a smile.

He picked the menu back up and scanned over it before it hit him. He placed the menu down and stood to his feet.

"What?" Tisha asked with a worried looked on her face.

"Why the fuck and who the fuck Candy here with?" he quizzed.

Goo stepped from around the table and scoped out the restaurant. It didn't take him long to spot Candy and some man near the back by the kitchen, engaged in conversation. He checked for his pistol before walking over to where they were.

"Now if I kill this nigga, you gon' be a witness, which means you can't represent me, so I might as well shoot the both of y'all," Goo spoke with nothing but venom spilling from his tongue.

"Look Rico, it's not like that?" Candy replied.

"Look shorty, it's *my* bad. *My bad*, I thought you were different from the rest of these bitches. Homie, y'all enjoy y'all dinner," Goo said, patting Lorenzo on the back before walking away.

When he made it back to the table, Tisha was preparing to order their food, but Goo interrupted her.

"Let's bounce, we can grab something somewhere else," he stated before walking towards the door.

"Oh ok?" a confused Tisha mumbled as she gathered her phone and purse.

Goo waited outside for her before he headed to car. Breathing the same air as Candy and that fuck nigga was going to make him catch a case. Goo thought about making a few calls that would result in Lorenzo being dead before he made it home but decided against it. He could tell by the look on that man's face that he was he innocent in it all, so he was going to spare him his life.

"Are you ok? What happened back there?" Tisha walked up, asking while placing her hand on Goo's shoulder.

"Nun man, it's good. I'm gotta get you back to your hotel. I gotta make some moves. Figure out what you want to eat and I'll get it," he replied, hitting the alarm to his Porsche truck.

"I'm actually ok. I'll order room service," she stated, getting inside the vehicle.

Without saying another word the entire ride, Goo pulled up to the front doors of the Marriot hotel twenty minutes later.

"I really appreciate you Tisha. And I'm sorry the night had to end so abruptly, but I'll get up with you before you head back to Atlanta."

"It's cool. I really wish you'll come up and take a shot with me. I mean, we are still celebrating," she replied, poking out her bottom lip for sympathy.

"You know what man, you right."

Goo pulled away from the door and found a parking spot not too far away. He cut the car off, grabbed his phone out the cup holder, and headed inside with Tisha. The two of them took the elevator to the fifth floor where her room was located. Once inside, Tisha cut on a few lights before heading over to the small bar right off the bathroom.

"I got Henny and Patron, what you like?" she asked, holding both bottles in the air.

"I need both them bitches, but I ain't trying to die tonight, so let me get a double shot of that Henny," he ordered.

"Coming right up!"

Goo watched Tisha make them both drinks, adding a few ice cubes to water them down just a little. He then watched her kick off the high heels she was wearing. Tisha walked over to where her purse was and pulled a rubber band from it, placing her hair in a high ponytail. He couldn't front, she was the *baddest* bitch in the neighborhood growing up, and years later, nothing has changed.

"To us, to years of friendship, to making it out the hood and doing well for ourselves," she handed Goo his glass, they both raised it in the air and toasted.

"Ahhhhhh!" Goo grimaced as the Hennessy burned his chest.

"Another one?" Tisha said as she took his empty glass and headed back to the bar.

"Shorty, you trying to get me drunk?" Goo asked, watching her fat ass move about in the dress she was wearing.

"Not at all friend. I told you, we are celebrating," she laughed, handing him his glass back.

Just like the time before, they toasted, but this time, Goo gave the speech.

"To being the only friend that never let me fuck. You the real MVP!" he stated, causing Tisha to laugh.

"You know I had to be different. You was fucking all the bitches from Homan to Pulaski," she replied.

"And I fucked you too… in my head. I used to jag off and think about you," Goo admitted.

"You a lie!" she laughed, playfully punching him in the arm.

"I swear to God. Beating the shit out my dick. Like this."

Goo took his hand and did the motions as if he was masturbating.

"I fucking hate youuuuuuuu!!!" Tisha said, hoovering over from laughter.

"I'm serious joe!" He replied, laughing along with her.

"Well guess what? We not kids anymore, and now you don't have to pretend."

Goo watched Tisha take a few steps back and pulled her dress down off her shoulders, eventually stepping completely out of it. He admired her perfect body, which was covered in just the right number of tattoos. She was perfect from her head to her toes, just like he remembered. Goo adjusted his dick in his pants and continued to stare at her. Tisha slowly walked over to where he was sitting in the chair and straddled him. Goo wrapped his arms around her, gripping her ass while she planted soft kisses on his neck.

"Goo, I want you to *fuck the shit* out of me," she whispered into his ear.

He picked her up by the waist and walked her over to the bed, where he sat her down. He looked at her one last time before walking towards the door.

"As bad as my dick *wanna* fuck the shit outta you, I can't," was all he said before exiting the room.

This was the first time in his twenty-five years on this Earth that his dick lost to his heart.

Chapter 27

Shit had been awkward between Kash and Mark for about the past week. It wasn't in a bad way; however, it was in a way that Mark really couldn't explain. The words that Goo spoke to him constantly rang in his head, so he knew that had a lot to do with it. It was true that he looked at Kash like a sister, but it would be a lie if Mark said that he never thought about her beyond that. It had been a minute since Mark had been to the gun range, so he texted Kash and told her that he was about to pick her up and take her. Mark was dressed in all black like he was ready for war, which he really was. The gun range was a place Mark frequented for various reasons. One was to blow off steam, another was to perfect his aim, but the current reason was to spend some more time with Kash. They bonded in the craziest ways, and it was time to add something new to the list.

Mark: Outside

Kash: On my way down

A few minutes later, Kash walked out of her building in all black. Mark admired her curves through her leggings. Kash had a body that a lot of women would pay for, but you wouldn't know it unless you were close to her because she always covered up. The sight of her in leggings made Mark's dick hard. He was glad that he had *super head* on standby because she had been coming in handy to him.

"Hey big head," she spoke after she hopped in.

"Hey big head to you too," he laughed.

"Somebody's in a good mood. You grinning all hard and shit," Kash assessed.

"I'm always in a good mood. You made it better though," Mark tested the waters.

"Hmm… likewise," Kash blushed.

Mark reached over and grabbed her hand and then kissed it before pulling away. He saw Kash trying her best to hold in a smile, but she couldn't hold it for long. Mark decided that it was time to talk and put everything out in the open. He took a deep breath as he drove and finally began.

"Have you ever looked at me as *relationship* type?"

"Yeah, but I didn't think you was interested really."

"How can a man *not* be interested in a woman as beautiful as you? I just knew that we both had been through shit and the friendship we built was so solid. I didn't wanna fuck it up. Ya feel me?"

"I get that... what's different now? You saying you wanna give it a try or you just talking?" Kash quizzed.

"You know I *don't* just talk. I been thinking long and hard about shit... about life. You're one that's gon' be in my life forever, and I think we owe it to ourselves to take that chance. I believe we can make it work. What you think?"

"I *know* we can make it work," Kash confidently replied.

"My girl... question though. Did you have any kinda feelings for Goo?"

"Nigga... nah. I was just messing wit' yo ass since you was entertaining hoes in front of me. You done dropped all your hoes though?" Kash shot back.

"Hoes? What makes you think I was entertaining hoes?" he chuckled and Kash shot him a *don't try to play me* look.

"Aight aight... I didn't have no hoes, but I was entertaining one hoe. She ain't shit for you to worry about though. You know how I get down," he confessed.

"You *better* make sure that whole situation is dead. You know I don't do the drama shit."

"Say no more," he replied and finally pulled up to the gun range.

Mark was happy about how the conversation had gone. If he had done that shit years ago, there was no telling what his life could have been like. That wasn't anything that he was going to dwell on though because his mom had always told them *whatever was meant to be will be*, and Mark believed her. His mom was always wise, and she let them know that everything happened for a reason. He still didn't know why God took her so soon, but Mark knew that he had a guardian angel looking over him.

They made their way to the stations and geared up. Mark never liked to put earpieces in, but it was a requirement, so he followed the rules. Him and Kash shot round after round and began making friendly bets with each other. It was crazy how everything felt so natural with her. Mark halfway expected shit to get awkward, but they were the same, and he knew that it would make their relationship that much stronger. Kash kicked his ass in the last round, and Mark blamed it on being hungry. After two hours, they decided to leave and go and grab a bite to eat. Before exiting, Mark grabbed Kash and pulled her close. His aim was to catch her off guard, and he did just that as he kissed her passionately. The way she kissed him back made him tingle all over. Mark hadn't ever felt that type of shit before. His dick grew in his pants, and he finally broke the kiss before he was tempted to bend Kash over and fuck her right then and there.

They made it back to his ride and got inside. Mark still had that kiss on his mind, and he could tell by the look on Kash's face that she did too.

"So that made it official huh?" she smiled.

"It was already official baby," he winked and then picked up his vibrating phone.

Mark noticed that he had five missed calls from *super head* and three text messages. The first two texts were messages about him not answering his phone, but the last text was like a gut punch to the stomach. Mark didn't know what to say or do, but he knew *damn well* that he had strapped up every single time that he was with her.

"You okay?" Kash asked him.

"Yeah… just gotta handle some shit."

There was no way that he could tell Kash that the hoe he had been fucking had just told him that she was pregnant.

Chapter 28

A few days had passed since Brandon arrived in Chicago, and Ebony was loving every minute of it. She received an email from her professor stating that he was planning to drop her if she missed one more day of class, which was yesterday. Brandon had fed her dreams about coming up in the world and her not needing college. He promised if she helped get the money from Goo, she'd never have to work another day in her life, and she believed him.

"So, you ready to put this plan in motion?" Brandon asked from the closet.

"Baby, I don't know. Are you sure that this will work?" Ebony asked doubtfully.

"Stop fucking asking me that stupid shit. Hell yeah it will work! The only way it won't is if you turn on me. You plan on turning on me?" he replied, walking towards her.

"I'll never but, it's just that….."

"It's just what?" Brandon yelled, causing her to jump.

"Nothing, I'll set it up."

"Cool, I'll be back, I'm about to run to the gas station up the street for some swishers," he told her before heading towards the door.

"I might be gone. Melissa is on her way to pick me up," she told him, but he ignored her and left out.

Ebony checked her phone to see if she had any messages before grabbing her Uggs and sliding them on. She tossed on her Northface hoodie and flopped on the bed, just in time to feel her phone vibrate. Ebony placed her thumb on the device to unlock it, reading a message from Melissa.

Melissa: Outside hoe ☺

Ebony didn't bother to reply, instead she grabbed the extra keycard off the table and headed downstairs. Once she was outside, she jumped into Melissa's ride and along with Kelsey, the three amigos headed to *Home Run Inn* to get some pizza. The entire ride, they rapped along to Cardi B's new album *Invasion of Privacy*. Ebony could listen to the album straight through, every song described something was that was currently going on in her life. It took them about an hour to get to the original *Home Run Inn* restaurant on 31st Street. They lucked up on a park near the door and headed inside. From all the cars in the parking lot, they thought it was going to be crowed, but they were immediately seated in a booth upstairs.

"So bitch, you been MIA since ya man been in town," Melissa wasted no time letting Ebony have it.

"Girl, all that nigga wanna do is fuck," Ebony blushed as she reminisced on her and Brandon's sex life.

"Aight keep it up. You gon' end up like this one here….." Melissa replied, pointing to Kelsey.

"This one here? What that mean? What you trying to say?" Ebony asked, her eyes darting back and forth between Melissa and Kelsey.

"Hello, I'm Amber and I'll be your host. Can I start you ladies off with drinks?" a young black girl with blonde weave asked.

"Actually, we ready to order. I want pizza, but I also have a taste for pineapples," Kelsey stated, her eyes never leaving the menu.

"BITCH WHAT? Ugh! Ain't nobody getting no pineapples on their pizza," Ebony shouted.

"I mean, I want them separately, is that possible?" she asked, looking up at the host.

"I'll see what I can do, I'll be back," the host replied before walking away.

Once she was gone, Melissa tore another asshole into Kelsey.

"Look bitch, we not finna start this pregnancy, craving shit," she snapped.

"Whoa! Whoa! Whoa! Who pregnant?" Ebony quizzed.

"Well… I took a test yesterday and it came back positive," Kelsey beamed.

"And who *the fuck* is the daddy?" Ebony questioned.

"Yeah… who the daddy?" Melissa repeated.

"Well, this nigga I been fucking with," she smiled.

"Names please?" Ebony insisted, pulling her phone from her pocket.

"Well, since you nosey hoes must know, his name is Mark," she finally killed the suspense.

"Mark who? Where he from?" Ebony inquired.

"He's from New York, but he's back in Chicago. Y'all, I *really* like this nigga, and I know he got bread."

"And you know this how? How much he give you?" Melissa asked with an attitude.

"Bitch about the same amount Goo gave you," Kelsey snapped.

"Aye y'all stop! Kelsey, I can't wait to meet this new man. I'm happy for you," Ebony said, trying her best to defuse the situation.

She was glad that the host reappeared to take their mind off the situation.

"Ok, I can get you side of pineapples for free. What else you ladies want?" she asked.

Ebony listened to Melissa and Kelsey place their order while she replied to a message that came through from Brandon.

Brandon: Did you handle that?

Ebony: Not yet…

Brandon: WHAT THE FUCK YOU WAITING ON???

Ebony left that last message on read and went into her text message inbox and scrolled until she came across Candy's name. She took a deep breath before shooting her a text.

Ebony: Hey cousin. My friend from school is having a party at Chuckie E Cheese for her son, and I wanted to know if I can take RJ with me? It's tomorrow at three.

While Ebony waited on a response, she ordered her some mozzarella sticks and a pink lemonade. Once the host took the menus, she checked her phone and like she had hoped, there was a message from Candy.

Candy: You sure can, he loves that place.

A smile invaded her face as she quickly texted Brandon back.

Ebony: We good to go. I'll have their son tomorrow around three.

Chapter 29

"I told you… I told you… I told you. You gon' learn to listen to me one of these days," Micah fussed.

"How many times you gon' say it?"

"As many times as I feel like, but I told you. That's why it took you so long to tell me," Micah shook her head.

"Okay okay okay… I fucked up. I admit that, but still… he broke up with me shit," Candy rolled her eyes.

They were walking through Rosemont, and it was crowded as hell, as expected for a Saturday. It had been a minute since the duo had been shopping, and since Ebony had taken RJ to one of her friend's little boy's birthday party at Chucky Cheese, Candy was taking advantage of the free time. The past few days, Candy had been working on RJ's upcoming birthday party, and she would be sure to tell Ebony to bring the little boy to celebrate with them. She wanted to go all out, but decided that she would keep it simple and do a Mickey Mouse themed party at the house. Candy couldn't believe that her baby was about to be one in six weeks. Time had really flown by.

"So have you talked to Lorenzo since then? I can visualize Goo telling you that 'you can't represent him if he kills buddy' because you'll be a witness. That nigga is a different kinda crazy," Micah laughed.

"He definitely is… and I still don't know why I love his ass so much," Candy sighed as she put a shirt against her body and looked in one of the mirrors to the right of her.

"You know why you love his ass… outside of the craziness, that nigga treats you like a queen, loves his son more than anything, and he takes care of home. He still has some growing to do, but he's waaayyy better than he was before. You gotta admit that."

Candy listened to what her friend was saying, and once again, she had to admit that Micah was right. Goo did a lot of shit, but the good outweighed the bad.

"You're right… but I still don't know about raising my son in this city anymore," Candy confessed.

"I can't argue with you on that. I got some years before I start having kids, but I can imagine I'm gonna feel the exact same way," Micah agreed.

"It's time for you to start having some babies now. I don't know what you waiting on."

"Girl whatever… Malik has hinted around about it, but he'll be okay. You didn't answer about Lorenzo though," Micah noted.

"Ohhh… girl I think he blocked me. Goo must have scared his ass, but little does he know, if Goo wanted to kill him, he woulda got him that night."

"I bet he did scare his ass. Why you think he blocked you? You called more than once?"

"Yep. It rings once and then goes straight to voicemail."

"Oh yeah, you blocked. What's his number?" Micah quizzed.

Candy gave her friend the number, and Micah dialed it and placed her phone on speaker. Lorenzo answered on the third ring, causing Micah to hang up the phone and bust out laughing.

"I would call him a *punk*, but I ain't gon' do it because Goo crazy," Micah continued laughing.

"Right," Candy agreed.

They went to a few more stores and bought more shoes and clothes. Micah bought a dress and a pair of Louboutins for her graduation next month. Candy saw a pair that Micah had been looking at and made a mental note to come back and get them for her girl as a graduation gift. She really admired her friend. The average woman would get with a nigga like Malik and do nothing but party and shop, but her friend was *more than* average, and she was so proud of her. She still helped her dad and sister out with the family business on top of going to school and taking care of the house she shared with her husband.

"You wanna get something to eat from here or go somewhere else?"

"With all these bags? We better get outta here and we can go to *Chipotle*? I been wanting a bowl from there for a few weeks now and just haven't been yet.

"Sounds good to me."

They made their way out of the mall with both bags on both of their arms. Micah was pushing her new white Bentley Bentayga that Malik bought her as an early graduation gift. They hopped in and threw their bags in the back and then Micah took off. *Irreplaceable* by Beyoncé came on. and Candy began singing along with her until Micah cut it off.

"What you doin' girl?" Candy quizzed.

"Turning this shit off before you do something stupid and Goo makes good on his threat," Micah laughed.

"Ugghhh… You so damn dramatic. Let me text him though."

Candy and Goo had still only been talking when it revolved around RJ, but she was tired of the back and forth. She decided to text him and say something that she hadn't said in a long ass time.

Candy: I love you!

She sent the text and then threw her phone down.

"What the hell you doin'?" Micah asked.

"You know how it be when you send a risky text… well that's what my dumb ass just did. Damn, can I take it back?" Candy said with her stomach in knots.

"And you called me *dramatic*," Micah shook her head and kept driving.

They pulled up to *Chipotle* about twenty minutes later. There was a vacant spot close to the front and Micah whipped into it. Candy picked her phone up and saw that Goo hadn't texted her back.

"I knew I shouldn't have texted that nigga. I should kick my own ass," she fussed as they got out.

As soon as she got out, her phone vibrated in her hand. She thought that it was Goo calling or texting, but it was Ebony. Candy would have let that call go to voicemail if her cousin didn't have RJ.

"Hey Eb... how's my ba..." she was cut off as she listened to Ebony tell her some fucked up news.

"*WHAT THE FUCK YOU MEAN RJ IS GONE?*" Candy screamed.

Chapter 30

"Nigga, why the fuck you smiling at yo phone like that?" Mark looked to the passenger's side and asked Goo.

"You all in a motherfucka business, but I'm smiling at a text from Candy," Goo replied.

Goo was pleasantly surprised at the "*I love you*" text from her. It had felt like forever since either of them uttered those words. They were still technically living in separate houses. Goo would spend a couple of nights out of the week with her when Candy had court in the mornings. He would get RJ up, dressed, and ready for daycare while she handled her business. He was thankful that she wasn't one of those miserable *bitter* baby mothers who just did shit out of spite, like keeping his son away from him. She never gave him a reason to think she was like that, but he knew women tended to switch up when shit went left.

"Y'all handle that shit?" Mark asked, referring the separation they were going through.

"Nah not yet, but I swear Ima make it right. Right after we handle this shit."

"So Timmy, I hope you got some good news for me," he stated, directing his attention to his worker who was sitting in the backseat.

Goo could hear Timmy blazing up the blunt. He used that time to text Candy back, but before he could send the message, his phone went dead. Goo checked the floor and armrest for his charger, forgetting that he left it in his other car.

"Niggaz catch a couple of bodies and get to running their mouths. They start to feel like a king because they were able to get so close to us," Timmy spoke before taking a hard pull from the blunt.

"Aight continue," Mark instructed, scrolling through his phone.

"Some nigga Lil P been pillow talking to is one of these hoes I be fucking. The nigga told her all about how he ran up in our spot. Gave her details in which only the motherfuckers there would know. What tripped me out was when she told me about the message he wrote in blood. This lil hoe said *you killed Lil P's daddy,* so now he's out to get you," Timmy explained, leaning forward and passing the blunt to Mark.

"*I killed his daddy?* I killed a lot of niggas' daddies. That ain't helping me none. Can you get the lil bitch on yo line?" Goo inquired.

Goo took the blunt from Mark while Timmy made the call. He didn't bother wrecking his brain trying to figure whose son that stupid motherfucker belonged to. Like he said, he was the reason a lot of motherfuckers hated Father's Day.

"Aye shorty, that nigga Lil P.... you know anything more about him or his pops?" Timmy asked.

"I told you all I know... oh and that his father dated Goo's mother. I think his pops was a pimp or something," the female recanted.

Goo dropped the blunt in his lap right after those words left her mouth. He quickly picked it up before it burned his interior.

"Aye baby girl. Do you know where I can find this nigga at? It's five thousand in it for you," Goo spoke aloud, so Timmy's girl could hear.

"*Hell yeah!* I'll text the address right now," she replied before ending the call.

"You know anything about that?" Mark asked.

"Yeah! The nigga who's after me is the son of the man who killed my OG," Goo explained.

"Huh?" Mark questioned.

"My OG was fucking with this nigga named Pimp when I was a shorty, and by shorty, I mean like fifteen. One day, some shit came up missing, and he blamed my OG for it. She told him that she ain't have shit to do with it, but he killed her anyway. He beat my mom's ass until she was unrecognizable. I came home that night, and there she was, lying in her own blood. I hit up Malik, and we went and found his ass like an hour later. Put one in his dome. *Damn!* That was my first body," Goo reminisced.

"And now on some revenge shit, his son coming after you," Mark stated.

"Which makes sense why he said that he's going to take yours since you took his," Timmy added in.

"Exactly!"

Goo stared out the front window in a daze. Flashbacks of his mother plagued his mind. He really didn't allow himself to relive that day, but it was shit like this that forced him to. He missed her like crazy, and she did whatever she had to do to ensure that he was straight. Candy reminded him so much of her; that's one of the reasons he loved her so much.

"Aye, buddy stay with his baby mother on Laporte and Westend," Timmy reported from the backseat.

"Nigga got the nerve to be in the hood acting reckless," Mark replied.

"Aye call Malik and see how close he is. Once I let this nigga know what's up, he gon' wanna make that move tonight," Goo said.

Mark pulled his phone out, preparing to call Malik as instructed.

"Here go his wife right here. Let me see what she want," Mark said, answering the phone for Micah.

"Hold on Micah. Calm down. Calm down. CALM DOWN!" He yelled, placing the phone on speaker.

"It's RJ! He's been *kidnapped*!" was the last thing Goo heard, along with Candy's screams before he mentally blanked out.

Chapter 31

Mark couldn't believe what he had just heard. If it wasn't one got damn thing, it was another. They had finally found out who had been after them, and it stemmed way back to the Pimp nigga that they killed. Hearing his name had put Goo in a frenzy and then getting a call that RJ was missing put the icing on the cake. Mark was about to pull off, but he looked to left and saw Kelsey pulling in. He had forgotten all about the fact that she was supposed to be sliding through. He didn't have time to entertain her, but it was a good thing he had Kash on standby. Instead of starting their relationship off with a lie, he told her the dilemma and she agreed.

"Let me handle her right quick," Mark told Goo.

"Hurry the fuck up… I gotta find my son," Goo fumed.

Mark knew that Goo was on ten thousand at the moment which was understandable, so he shot Kash a text as he got out to let her know what was up right before Kelsey made her way to him.

"We got an emergency right now, so Ima have to get up wit' you later," Mark started and then Goo's voice boomed, causing Kelsey to jump.

"Nigga… Micah just called and said somebody took RJ. He was at a party at *Chucky Cheese* with Ebony… yeah… we finna head to the crib now. Bet," Goo hung up, and Mark knew that he had to be talking to Malik to give out that kind of information over the phone.

"Did he say Ebony took his baby to a party? Whose party?" Kelsey quizzed.

Mark wanted to tell her to mind her business, but the way she said *that* made him feel as if she knew something.

"You know Ebony?" he quizzed.

"Yeah… we be hanging out. She kinda ditched us for her lil boyfriend lately though."

"So which one of y'all got kids?"

"Neither of us… none that lived anyway," Kelsey mumbled, and Mark couldn't help but to think that little did she know, the one that *she* was carrying wouldn't live either, if she was telling the truth.

He saw Kash walking up, and he motioned for her to come on. Kelsey looked back and saw Kash. Mark saw her mood change instantly.

"Kelsey… this is Kash, *my woman*. She gon' explain to you how this shit gon' go down," he told Kelsey before turning to Kash and telling her on what to do next. "Baby, handle that and call me ASAP. We got another situation," Mark told her and hopped back into his car.

Mark had instructed Kash on exactly what to do. He knew good and well that he had never slept with Kelsey without protection, so if she was *really* pregnant, she had done some shady type shit or the baby wasn't his. Kash would get it out of her. He was smart enough to know that it all boiled down to money any damn way, and he was prepared to pay. He pulled away and headed towards Candy and Goo's crib.

"Nigga… Kelsey knows Ebony, and she said Ebony ain't even got no friends with kids. You think she on some *foul* type shit?"

"I don't know. but we damn shol' 'bout to find out."

Mark maneuvered though the streets of his city with a mind full of thoughts. Goo was quiet as hell, but Mark knew that somebody was about to feel his wrath soon and very soon.

"Mu'fuckas must don't know who the fuck *Rico Goo Grady* is!! I shoulda known that bitch Ebony was foul too. That hoe got my money and lied about the got damn chump change. This all my fault for being in these streets too much like Candy been fussing about. FUCK!!" Goo vented.

"Bruh… we gon' get RJ back, and you and Candy gon' be straight. Just focus."

Mark saw Goo reach into the bag on the floor and grab the bottle of *Henny* that they had been drinking from earlier before the other shit surfaced. He practically poured the liquor down his throat, and Mark grabbed the bottle from him and drank some too. He pulled up to Goo's crib thirty minutes later, and Goo ran to the door. Mark didn't waste any time catching up. Goo busted through the door, and Ebony was sitting on the couch with her phone in her hands while Micah was consoling a crying Candy. Goo headed straight to Ebony before Mark could stop him.

Chapter 32

Micah did her best to console her friend, but Candy felt like she was about to lose it at any minute. Ebony told her that she was about to head home, so Candy told Micah to head to her house. Candy couldn't help but to start blaming herself.

"I never should have let him go. I don't even know Ebony's friends. What was I thinking?"

"No Candy. You are not about to start blaming yourself. Shit happens. Ebony should have been more fucking responsible anyway. If it's anybody's fault, it's *hers*, but for now, we are gonna remain calm. We *will* get RJ back. Goo and Malik, along with us, will paint this city *red*, and you know it," Micah told her.

Candy got quiet. She knew that Micah was right, but she still felt like a bad mother. Her mind was in a blur the rest of the ride home. Before she knew it, Micah was parking. Candy got out and rushed inside, in hopes that Ebony was already there. She had some questions to ask, and she needed answers *immediately*.

"Ebony! Ebony!" Candy yelled, but found out that Ebony wasn't there.

"You think she called the police?" Candy asked Micah when she walked in.

"I hope not… no cops until we find out more info," Micah informed her.

"See, that shit right there is why…"

"Not right now Candy… not right now."

Candy sighed in frustration and continued pacing the floor. She pulled her phone out and called Ebony, but she didn't answer. Just when she was about to call again, the door flew open and Ebony rushed in.

"I'm so sorry Candy," Ebony cried and ran to her.

"Tell us *exactly* what happened!!" Micah demanded, and Candy saw the look that Micah and Ebony both gave each other.

It was clear that they didn't like each other, but it was time to put their differences to the side, put their heads together, and find RJ. That was exactly what Candy told them. Ebony ran the story down to them about how RJ was having a great time and enjoying himself. She said that she placed him in the high chair to go and get some coins, and when she came back, he was gone. Candy listened, but she still couldn't process anything.

"So where were your friends? What are their names? Did you call the cops?" Micah fired questions back to back to back.

"No, I didn't call the cops because I see what kinda lives Candy and Goo living," Ebony rolled her eyes at Micah.

"So you just ignore the first two questions. *This* bitch foul Candy," Micah stepped towards Ebony.

"Wh… what?" Ebony stuttered.

"You heard what the fuck I said."

"Bitch… you just don't like me because I can take yo man… you using this opportunity just to…"

Before Ebony could finish her sentence, Micah had slapped the shit out of her. Before Ebony could react, Micah punched her in the face and pushed her down.

"Micah… this isn't helping," Candy pulled her friend off of her cousin.

"Bitch… Ima beat yo ass," Ebony yelled.

"Both of y'all chill the fuck out!! *PLEASE!!*" Candy screamed.

The only thing that could be heard in the room was heavy breathing from Micah and Ebony. Part of Candy wanted to let Micah beat the fuck out of Ebony because something wasn't right. She switched from *mommy mode* to *lawyer mode* just that fast and started asking her cousin questions. She fired them constantly and was going to ask those same questions again in a different way shortly. It wasn't that she didn't want to believe her cousin, but something just wasn't right. Candy walked to the bathroom and grabbed a fresh face towel out of the cabinet. She turned the cold water on, wet it, and then wet her face. A fresh batch of tears ran down Candy's face. She cried silently and then left the bathroom and went to RJ's room.

"He's gonna be okay. I promise you," Micah appeared behind her as she stared at the different pictures of her son on the wall.

"I need my son, Micah. I need him to be okay."

"Goo is on his way. Come on let's go back in here and wait on him."

"She's lying, isn't she?" Candy asked in reference to Ebony.

"I damn sure think she is," Micah confirmed.

"I'm gonna find out shortly."

They made their way back to the living room, and Candy started pacing the floor again.

"I can make a phone call and get the surveillance from the restaurant. Let me do that now," Candy said out of nowhere.

"I already talked to them," Ebony spoke up.

Out of nowhere, one of RJ's toys started singing, and it made Candy cry. Micah walked over to her and pulled her in for a hug. The door flew open a few minutes later and Candy looked up and saw Goo heading straight for Ebony, who was on her phone texting or something.

"What friend of yours had this party?" Goo fumed.

"Melissa," Ebony answered, causing Candy to look up because she had just said earlier that it was someone named *Kelsey*.

"So *Melissa* got a baby?"

"Yeah."

"How old is the baby??" Goo asked.

"He... he turned two."

"So you telling me, Melissa got a two year old and that's whose party you took my son to?"

"Yeah… I met her at school and we been close since the first day."

"*Kelsey* said her *and* Melissa ain't got *no* muthafuckin' kids though," Goo raged.

Candy watched as Ebony's eyes got big as fuck. They got even bigger when Goo pulled his pistol out. Before anyone could do anything, Goo fired one shot that made Ebony hit the floor.

Chapter 33

"Oh my God! Goo noooo!" Candy screamed out as Ebony fell to the ground.

"Listen *bitch*, we finna play a game. I ask you a question, and every time you *lie*, you get a bullet. Ready?" Goo smirk as he bent over in Ebony's face.

"No Goo! Stop! Give her time to talk," Candy pleaded, placing her hand on his shoulder.

"Where the fuck is my son?" he asked, completely ignoring Candy.

"I – don't – know," Ebony cried.

"That's a bullet for you!" he said, this time shooting her in the arm.

Ebony screamed out in pain. She didn't know whether to aid her arm or her leg, but no one in the room felt sorry for her.

"GET THE FUCK UP!" Goo yelled, ignoring the look of pain Ebony gave him.

"NOW BITCH!" he yelled again.

Ebony grabbed onto the couch and pulled herself up with the good arm. She cried out and pleaded, but it fell on death's ears. Everyone stood around, waiting for Goo's next move.

"Where that nigga at?" Goo asked.

"What nigga?" she cried.

Goo took the butt of his gun and hit Ebony upside the head, causing blood to leak on contact.

"This is my *last* motherfucking time asking you anything. Where the fuck is my son?" he yelled.

"I am so sorry. *Candy*, I'm sorry. RJ is at the hotel with Brandon. Brandon promised not to hurt him. We just needed money and didn't know what to do," she sobbed from the hurt and pain that she was feeling and from having to disclose the truth.

"So *you* kidnap my fuckin' son!" Candy screamed, charging at Ebony, who fell back onto the floor.

Both Candy, along with Micah, stomped Ebony wherever they saw an opening. Ebony tried her best to cover her face, leaving the rest of her body open for blows.

"STOP Y'ALL!" Goo ordered, pulling them off of her.

"Get the fuck up and take me to RJ," he demanded to Ebony.

Goo, Candy, Mark, Micah, along with a limping and bloodied Ebony, headed out the front door. As soon as they hit the porch, Malik came flying down the street in his black Maserati. He didn't allow the car to stop fully before he jumped out.

"Where the fuck is RJ?" he asked, looking around at everyone.

"*This* bitch had her boyfriend kidnap him," Micah said, staring a hole through Ebony.

Before anyone knew it, Malik pulled his pistol from his waist and placed it upside her head.

"Bitch, if my Godson has a scratch on him, I'm blowing yo motherfuckin' brains out," Malik spoke closely to Ebony's ear through clenched teeth before placing his gun back on his hip.

"Let's go get my baby," Candy said, walking to the car.

The crew all got into their respective cars and headed to the Marriott hotel, which was about ten minutes away. Goo made sure that Ebony was placed in the car with him, so he could keep a close eye on her. He didn't care that she was leaking blood all over his seats or anything. His main focus was to get to his son as quick as possible. He drove while Mark sat in the backseat with her, with his pistol on his lap. Goo drove like a bat of hell. He didn't want to take any chances on something happening to his boy. Not bothering to find a park, he killed the engine right at the front door.

"Bitch throw this on," he said, tossing Ebony a hoodie to cover up her bleeding arm, just in case they ran into some nosey motherfuckers.

"And *stop* all that motherfucking crying. Yo ass gon' die anyway," Mark added in as they all made their exit.

Ebony led them to the fifth floor. They walked down the long hallway until they reached room 523. Once there, Ebony paused and looked behind her.

"Knock bitch!" Micah ordered, pushing her in the back.

Ebony did what she was told, knocking three times. RJ's cries could be heard from the other side, which made Goo's blood boil even more.

"He's hurting my baby," Candy broke down.

"Shhhhhhhh…" Mark said, placing his index finger to his mouth.

Candy immediately silenced her cries, and a few seconds later, Brandon's voice could be heard.

"Who is it?"

"It's me…. It's me," Ebony replied with broken words.

A few seconds later, the door swung open and the only thing Goo saw was the back of Brandon's head. The nigga had the nerve to just open the door and walk away like shit was sweet.

"This motherfucking baby won't stop crying. This shit killing me," Brandon said, leading them to the bedroom where RJ was laying on the bed, crying his eyes out.

"Nigga, you should have been thought about that!"

Brandon turned around so fast, you would have thought he would have got whiplash. His eyes grew the size of golf balls when he noticed Goo, Mark, Micah, and Malik with their guns drawn. Candy took that opportunity to grab their son. She picked him up and did a quick look over him before joining the gang.

"So let's play a game. I'll let Ebony give you the rules since she plays so well," Goo spoke up.

"Baby, *I am so sorry*…. I never meant for none of this to happen," Ebony looked over at Brandon and cried.

"Question number one. Did you really think it'll be a good idea to snatch up my son?" Goo asked.

Brandon stood there frozen. You could tell that he hadn't planned on things turning out like this. He looked around at the four guns pointed to him but still didn't speak.

"So there's a time limit on how long you can take to answer and the buzzer just went off," Goo said, taking his gun and aiming it at Brandon's foot before letting off a shot.

Brandon let out a strings of cuss words as the pain radiated off his foot. He started hopping around like that would stop the bleeding or pain. Before he could ask for help, Goo had already asked his next question in the game.

"Now my next question, who you want to die first?" he quizzed.

Both Ebony and Brandon locked eyes, causing Goo to let out a sinister laugh.

"Look, I know this is a difficult choice, so I'll decide for y'all," he said, twisting the silencer on his gun tighter.

"Look bruh, I can explain," Brandon finally spoke, but it was a little too late.

"Mannnn… shut the fuck up!" Goo replied before raising his gun and shooting Brandon in the middle of his forehead.

Before Ebony could let out a scream, she had a matching hole in the middle of hers.

Chapter 34

Candy couldn't believe how that shit had played out. Her own cousin tried to play her for some money. She was in the backseat of Micah's car holding RJ's hand as he slept. Candy and RJ got in with Micah since RJ's seat was already in her vehicle. Goo was in front of them, and Candy couldn't wait until all of them were safely inside of their home. RJ hadn't been hurt in any type of way, thank God, but Candy's nerves were still on ten. Candy closed her eyes and took a deep breath. Out of nowhere, gunfire rang out, and she felt the car swerve as Micah screamed. Candy reached and threw her arms around RJ by instinct.

"Are y'all okay?" Micah panicked and pulled the car over off the highway.

"I think so… yeah. What about you? What the hell happened? Where's Goo?"

Micah's silence made Candy start panicking that much more. Something was terribly wrong, Candy could feel it. She looked out the car's window and saw Goo's car flipped over and Candy screamed.

"Oh my God!! NOOOO!!"

Candy hopped out of the car and took off running. She looked at his car, and it was filled with bullet holes. Candy heard Micah calling out to her, but she had to get to Goo. Micah would keep RJ, that much she was sure of. When Candy made it to Goo, all she saw was blood. He was halfway out of the car, and from what she could tell, he looked lifeless. Candy fell down by his side crying. In the distance, Candy heard sirens, but she was so out of it, she didn't know that the paramedics had arrived until someone grabbed her. She looked up and saw the EMT's and Micah standing right behind them holding RJ.

"Come on Candy. Let them do their job, and we'll meet them at the hospital."

Candy followed Micah back to the car. She honestly didn't know how she made it because she was in a daze. She listened as Micah told her that she saw a black car pull up beside Goo and open fire. All Candy could think about was how she always said the street shit was going to be the death of them.

"Ma… ma!"

RJ's voice snapped her back to reality, and it made her start back crying. Candy was over the crying shit. She had shed enough tears within the past few weeks to last a lifetime. The image of Goo's bloody body was etched in her mind. She couldn't do shit to shake it. Candy instantly started praying. It had been a minute since she had been to church, but she knew that God knew her heart.

"Be careful baby… please?" Micah said, and Candy knew that she was talking to Malik.

Candy held RJ the entire trip. She was one of those people who hated seeing kids not in their car seats, but at that moment, she just needed to hold her son close. Micah pulled up at Rush and they got out. When they ran in, Micah took RJ from Candy, and she went straight to the admissions desk. She was informed that Goo was in bed three and a doctor or nurse would be out to speak with them as soon as they had any information. Candy knew how shit went, so she sucked it up and went and sat down. She feared the worst. The longer they sat there, Candy continued thinking the worst.

"My son got kidnapped and his daddy *might* be dead. I can't do it anymore Micah. *I just can't.* Chicago just can't be home for me anymore."

"Goo is as tough as they come. Stop thinking the worst boo," Micah rubbed her leg.

"Did you… did you see him lying there? In all that blood?" Candy got choked up.

Micah got quiet, and Candy finally looked up and made eye contact with her. She saw the tears in her friend's eyes, and she could tell that she was feeling the same exact way as her. Micah was being a great friend and was trying to be strong. Candy appreciated her for it, but at that moment, she needed the truth.

"I did see him, but we still have to be strong and positive. Goo isn't going to leave you two," Micah comforted her.

"Any word on my mans?" Malik busted through the door with Mark not too far behind.

"Not yet... hopefully it won't be much longer. Are y'all okay?" Micah asked them.

"That all depends on my mans... fuck! I should have been right in there with him."

"Goo gon' be straight... everybody just calm down," Mark spoke up.

They gathered themselves as best as they could. Mark grabbed RJ and began playing with him. He was oblivious to the situation that was happening, and it seemed as if he momentarily shed some light into a dark situation. Candy looked up and saw a doctor heading their way. Her stomach was already in knots, but the shit felt like a pretzel to her at that moment. She could tell that everyone followed her eyes because they all got quiet.
"Are you all the family of Mr. Rico Grady?" he asked and Candy shook her head *yes*.

"Well... this is hard to explain, but..."

That was all the doctor got out before a *code red* to bed three was called, and he instantly disappeared. Candy couldn't hold it together any longer because she knew that was Goo's bed. Everything around her faded black.

Chapter 35

Three Months Later

Candy stepped out into her backyard and the sun was beaming. RJ was playing in the kiddie pool and having a ball. Right after his birthday party, Candy took her son and moved down south. Since she had passed the bar for the state of Georgia years ago, she applied for some jobs and was offered several positions instantly. The pay was even surprisingly better for it to be in the south, and Candy wasn't going to start until the day after Labor Day. She had a few months to relax and regroup. It hurt her to leave Chicago, but she felt like she didn't have a choice. A fresh start was needed.

She went and splashed some water on RJ, making him laugh. Thoughts of Goo entered Candy's mind and she almost cried. She wished that he was there with them so bad, but the cards just didn't fall that way. Her phone started ringing, and she knew that it was Micah because *Best Friend* by Brandy was playing. Candy ran and grabbed her phone and answered the FaceTime call.

"Heeyyy," she sang.

"Hey boo… oh y'all outside chillin' and shit. I'm jealous," Micah pouted.

"Stop playing… I'm waiting on you to come back. I can't thank y'all enough for helping me get settled in."

"Really Candy… that's what family does. I know it was hard for Malik to do, but he managed. I'm coming back sooner than you think though," Micah smiled.

"I can't wait… it's sooo peaceful here. Sometimes it scares me not hearing sirens and shit twenty-four seven," Candy chuckled.

"Ohhh… did you find out what happened with Mark and that *Kesley* chick?" Candy asked.

"Giiirrrllll… Kash made that bitch disappear. *That* bitch is the truth!" Micah bragged.

"Dammnnn… well, I suppose things are great between her and Mark right?"

"Yeah they all in love and shit. It's so cute. I think I'll have a new sister soon," Micah admitted.

"That's sweet. He deserves it. Girl, let me take RJ inside. He looks like he's getting sleepy."

"Okay. Be sure you call me back."

Candy hung up the phone and then went and picked up her son. His head fell on her shoulders instantly. She knew that he was sleepy by how quiet he had gotten. Candy picked up the towel and wrapped it around him. It appeared that giving him a bath first was out of the question, so she went and laid him down on the chaise so that she could whip up something quick for them to eat. When Candy turned to go to the kitchen, her doorbell rang. She had no idea who it could be because her people were in Chicago and Michigan. Candy even bought a house in a gated community, so she figured it had to be a neighbor. She opened the door and butterflies formed in her stomach when she saw Goo down on his knees, holding the biggest rock that she had ever seen in her life. Tears instantly began to run down her cheeks.

"You knew I was coming. I just had to take care of shit so that you and my son could be safe. Ain't gon' be no more of that back and forth shit. I love *the hell* outta you, and I want you to be my wife and have the rest of my kids. Will you marry me?"

"Yes… of course I will," Candy cried, and Goo slipped the ring on her finger.

He picked her up and kissed her passionately. Candy felt his dick growing in his pants and she knew what time it was. She was in need because she hadn't had any since before she left Chicago. Before they could make it to the room, RJ must have felt the presence of his dad because he woke up. The smile that appeared on both RJ and Goo's faces warmed Candy's heart. At that moment, she knew that everything was well and she had to thank God for sparing Goo's life and giving her lil family a second chance.

The End.

Made in the USA
Monee, IL
29 July 2022

10535791R00095